LUCIFER'S TIPPLE

LUCIFER'S TIPPLE

LEO MILLIER

Leo Millier
Lucifer's Tipple

All rights reserved
Copyright © 2025 by Leo Millier

Published by Spines

ISBN: 979-8-89691-249-1

CONTENTS

CHAPTER I

On a lovely autumn afternoon. The air was crisp and fresh. Sebastien was in a nice pub. It was old-fashioned. All hardwood panelling, oak beams and large fireplaces. It's like a country pub but in the heart of the city. And not rowdy like some. This has a quiet buzz to it. An energy. Created by the relaxed conversations that filled the space. Altogether, it created an atmosphere of coziness.

Sinking into a leather armchair. With a pint. By a roaring fire. He was relaxed. Calm. After a busy week at the practice. He could now unwind. The weekend had arrived.

"So, you will come. Won't you?"

His plans of generally doing nothing, however, are becoming more and more unlikely.

"But. Why do you want me to go?"

Sebastien challenged.

"Come on. It will be fun."

Archie replied.

"Fun?"

Sebastien said. Doubtfully.

"You are so keen for a friend to go with you to a family gathering. Because you think it will be fun?"

"Yes. Listen. You will enjoy it. It's a charming house in Dartmoor. Great food and drink. What more do you want?"

"Dartmoor?"

"Yes. Dartmoor."

Archie confirmed.

"The National Park. Surely, you would love to see it."

"Yes. I am sure it is a lovely place."

Sebastien agreed.

"But if I were going to visit, I would do it myself. On holiday. I would not just turn up at a stranger's house, someone I have never met, and demand bed and board."

"They are not strangers. They are my family. So do not be ridiculous. They will be thrilled to have you."

Sebastien sighed. Looking opposite. Sat in a chair. Identical to his own. Was his friend. With ginger hair. A freckled face. A short but slim build. He had a certain schoolboy charm about him. A mixture of cuteness and cheekiness. In contrast to Sebastien's chiselled jaw, clear skin and neat black hair. It was as if Archie's growth had paused in his teenage years.

Sebastien was incredibly fond of him. His energy and enthusiasm. They made him infectious. Someone you gravitate towards. Normally, however, he was transparent. One of the most genuine people he knew. Truly wearing his heart on his sleeve. Today, however, he was not being completely truthful. Sebastien could see it in him, in his eyes.

"Be honest. Why do you really want me to come?"

Archie frowned. He shrugged, falling back into his chair. "Ok. Truthfully. I am not looking forward to it. You see, I do not know them that well. So I want a friendly face to keep me company. Alright."

"Oh. So, you thought you would trick me? Make me suffer this dreadful, awful experience as well?"

Sebastien replied with a hint of offence in his voice.

Archie smirked, clearly amused.

"It was not like that. I think that both of us going would make it enjoyable. We can entertain ourselves. Otherwise, I just think I will get bored stiff with people I do not really know."

"Entertain ourselves?"

Asked Sebastien.

"I am not sure what activities you have in mind. Not sure I want to."

He was smirking now.

"Oh. Shut up."

Archie replied.

"I just mean we can talk. Hang around. Maybe explore a bit of Dartmoor. Just be with each other."

"What about your family? Surely there must be some people you like that you get along with?"

Archie shrugged.

"Uncle Tony is alright, I guess. Pretty friendly. Aunt

Imogen, though. God. She is so stuck up. I just know she will look down on me. Think the business is a waste of time."

"How is your business going?"

Sebastien asked, interested.

"Well…"

Archie replied slowly.

"It is a bit slow to pick up, but it will. It just needs time."

Sebastien smiled and nodded. Archie had started a venture into alcohol. Craft beer. Not a bad business to get into. But competitive. Turning it from a hobby into a successful business was not easy. As Archie was learning. Then there was the taste. He was no expert. But he had tried some. Under duress. And he thought it needed a bit of improvement. To put it mildly. Yes, it needed work. But trying things and seeing what works. That seems to be how you do it. How you build a business. Archie would get there. Eventually. The thing that concerned Sebastien was how many rounds of 'testing' he would be required to do. At this rate, he might end up passing out.

"Do not try to change the subject. Come to Dartmoor."

Said Archie. Pulling him back into the moment.

"I did not. You mentioned it. Okay. What about your cousin? I think you have mentioned her before. She is younger. Surely you would like to see her?"

Archie grimaced.

"Rebecca. She has bad vibes."

"Bad vibes?"

Sebastien pressed.

"What do you mean?"

"I mean, she is just so focused. So ambitious. You just always get the feeling that she is not really interested in you, only what she can get from you. That she would trample you to get what she wanted."

Sebastien exhaled.

"Alright. Who else is going to be there? Surely there are others you want to see?"

Archie thought.

"There is Jessica. She is nice. Fun and bubbly. She is Aunt Imogen's Niece. Has been with them since her parents died. Some car accident."

Sebastien nodded.

"Ok. Anyone else?"

Archie exhaled deeply.

"Well, there is another niece with her husband, some of Rebecca's friends. The problem is I do not know them. I only see Uncle Tony occasionally, and these people are never there. I never see Aunt Imogen's side of the family or Rebecca's friends. The problem is it's her birthday party. It is all people that I do not know."

"Her birthday party! Oh great. So now I am not just going to a stranger's house; I am gatecrashing a birthday party. What's next? A wedding?"

"Calm down. You are not gatecrashing anything. I was invited. You are simply my plus one. That is all."

"Archie, a plus one, is for a romantic partner. A date. Not a friend."

"Well, they have always thought I am quite liberal. They will probably just not ask. Who knows? Maybe we will discover a hidden love for each other. It is a very romantic place."

Sebastien frowned.

"Haha. Very Funny. Look. Why don't you just say you're busy? That the business needs you. You cannot get away. Surely, they would understand that?"

"Well. To tell you the truth, when I spoke to Uncle Tony, he sounded really keen for me to come. I do not want to disappoint him. A wealthy relative is always useful."

Sebastien fixed him with a look.

"So that's it. You want to get money off him?"

"No. Not necessarily. There just may be a time when the business expands. Potential investors are useful to know. And there is the will to consider."

"You know. Your concern. It brings tears to my eyes."

Sebastien teased.

Archie shrugged.

"Listen. We are not close. We only see each other once a year, usually. I am just looking towards the future. That is all."

"Ok. Well. Why don't you ask someone else, like Kiera or Jasper? Perhaps they would like to go?"

"What do you think I tried first? I knew they would be easier to convince than you. They are both busy."

He paused.

"Please come. I promise you will enjoy it."

Sebastien looked at him skeptically.

"You promise I will enjoy it. Okay, how? How exactly can you promise that I will enjoy it?"

Archie hesitated for a moment, trying to find the right words.

"Because I will be there."

He said cautiously.

Sebastien fell back in a mock state of shock; a stunned expression was on his face.

"Oh wow. I never realized that. Oh, that changes everything."

He said sarcastically.

"You know, I thought you were just going to drop me off while you went on a two-week holiday to Ibiza."

"Well, it would."

Replied Archie defensively.

"We would have fun together."

Changing to a softer tone, Archie said.

"Come on. I mean, what else do you have planned for this weekend? What else exactly are you doing that's so important?"

Sebastien hesitated for a moment.

"Bake-off."

"What?"

Archie asked.

"You heard me. Bake off. I am planning to watch Bake Off."

"That is not a plan."

Archie challenged.

"That is a TV show."

"Yes. One I plan to watch. I want to lay on my sofa. Watch Bake Off. Eating cake. There. You happy?"

"Did you bake the cake?"

Archie asked, struggling to stifle a laugh.

"No. I have been working."

Sebastien replied stiffly.

"Goodness gracious. Paul would be disappointed."

Archie said, unable to contain his laughter any longer.

Sebastien made a face. Unamused.

"Listen. Plans do not have to be with other people. I want to have a pint with you today. And tomorrow, watch the Bake Off. I want to relax. Unwind. I have some time to myself. What is wrong with that?"

"Nothing really."

Archie replied, coming out of his laughing fit.

"I was only joking. You should bake a cake, though. Then I can try some."

He paused.

"There is one thing, though."

"What?"

"You cannot really say, You are having a pint."

"What do you mean? Yes, I am."

"Pineapple juice does not count!"

"It is the same colour."

Sebastien replied casually.

"And it tastes better."

"Better than this pale ale. Come off it."

"We are getting distracted. The point is, I have plans for this weekend. I cannot come with you."

"Well. They are not set in stone, are they? I mean, you could reschedule your bake-off session."

Sebastien looked up at the ceiling, exhausted.

"God. You are not going to give up, are you?"

"Nope."

Archie confirmed.

"Look, please come."

He pleaded.

Sebastien gave him a sympathetic look.

"It is beautiful surroundings. Great food. Nice enough, people. It will be great. Come on. Please."

After a pause, Archie added.

"It would really help me out."

Sebastien sighed deeply.

"Alright. Fine."

He said reluctantly.

"Great. Thank you. You will not regret this. I will pick you up at three."

Dammit, Sebastien thought. I was looking forward to that Victoria sponge.

CHAPTER 2

Walking away from the pub, Archie was pleased with himself. He knew Seb would come around eventually. All it took was some gentle persuasion. Okay, a lot of persuasion. But he would enjoy it, really. And it would be good for him. Getting out of the city. Getting some country air. That is what they say, don't they? Yes. Archie's weekend had certainly improved. His persistence had paid off.

Walking back to his flat, he thought about the weekend ahead. He just hoped it would be pleasant. You never really knew what to expect when going to Uncle Tony's. The atmosphere could be light and breezy or as cold as ice.

Uncle Tony was alright. He was the definition of a charmer, perhaps right to the line of what would be called slimy. But just not crossing it. The point was he was always friendly. With his big smile and easy conversation. He would be good company.

Aunt Imogen, on the other hand, well, sometimes she was pleasant. Asking how you were doing. What were you up to? Like a concerned grandmother. But sometimes, it just felt like she was judging you constantly. Prying into your life. Rooting out your failures. Judging your mistakes. As if I am somehow unworthy of her family. Hopefully, she will be in a favourable mood.

Then there is Rebecca. Well, as I already said, bad vibes. It is not that she is unpleasant. On the contrary, she is friendly enough. It's perfectly normal, really. It is just that there is this sense, this feeling of selfishness and ruthlessness. Frankly, from what I have heard, she would sell our own grandmother to make a partner. But this should not be a problem. We are not trying to take anything from her. We are not a threat. So, she should be fine.

I guess that leaves Jessica. She is nice. Young, slim and blonde. Always up for a laugh. Oh god. Her laugh. It is like a proper schoolgirl, high-pitched one. Bubbly. That is the right word to describe her. Yes, Bubbly. The point is she will be nice to have around. We can chat and have a joke. Yes. She really is a great girl. I must admit when I first met her. I was rather taken. She is rather stunning. But I quickly got that out of my head. Even Uncle Tony would draw the line there. And can you imagine Aunt Imogen? If looks could kill. I would be buried on the moor. No. Best to leave that one. No matter.

As for the rest of the party, I am not really sure. As I said. I do not see Uncle Tony often. These other people are never there. There is another cousin, I believe. Not sure about the name. A nurse, I think, and her husband. I do not know much about him. Yes, I think they are coming.

There are also Rebecca's friends. Again, I don't really know anything. I think they all grew up together in Dartmoor. Apart from that, I am none the wiser.

You see, this is why I did not want to go alone. I barely know most of them. Out of those I do know, there is Uncle Tony. Decent company. But I cannot stick to him all weekend. Then there is Aunt Imogen. If I stuck to her, I might freeze to death. Then there are Rebecca and Jessica. They will be more interested in their friends than me. So, you see, having Seb with me will make it all less awkward. Yes, it will certainly make it bearable. And who knows? He may even enjoy it.

I do feel a bit guilty. I have taken over his weekend. And I get it. He is an introvert. He's quiet. He needs time to himself to recharge. Now and then, he needs to be by himself, away from everyone else. From me. And I respect that. He is my friend. I like him just the way he is and would never change him. But it would not hurt him to get out there a bit more. Just sometimes. I know he is not going to be clubbing at 5 a.m., but maybe it is good he is going to be with people. Mingling. Socialising. That being said, he is a therapist. He does listen to people all day. Perhaps I am just trying to make excuses to myself to make myself feel better for forcing him to come. No. He will enjoy it. I will make sure of it. If it gets too much. We can go for a walk or something. And in the end, I need him. I cannot do this on my own.

I know he is not keen. And really. I know bringing him is more for myself then him. But he may like it. I mean. The food is always good. They always have great caterers for these things. The drink is decent. And the house is comfortable. Good mattresses. Soft carpets. Central heating. He will not be uncomfortable while he is there. And who knows? He may find it interesting. As a psychotherapist, after all. Maybe he will enjoy seeing it all unfold. Observing our behaviour. Diagnosing the countless problems that we have in the family. And if it gets too much. We can go for a wander. Just in the grounds. Or even onto Dartmoor itself.

It is beautiful down there. The rugged landscape. Hills covered in huge, craggy rocks. It does have a certain adventure to it. A feeling that you are in the wilderness. Remote. Alone in the world. Perhaps we will go wild. Abandoning civilization. Like native tribesmen. No, perhaps not. I cannot see Sebastien even going camping. No matter him going native. But it would be a good escape, though. Yes. Perhaps we should do some walking. We can get away from the family and enjoy the beautiful scenery. And it is all socially acceptable. Perfect.

Getting closer to his flat now, Archie is aware of the time. He only has an hour until he is collecting Sebastien. He needs to shower, change, and pack. Their train leaves only half an hour after. Perhaps he should have gotten a later ticket. Oh well. I can't change it now.

Hurrying there, he is focused on getting ready for the journey ahead.

CHAPTER 3

The kitchen at Clayton's is every housewife's dream: a large room with marble worktops lining the edges. Coloured light grey with dark, cracking streaks for effect. A large agar is set against the back wall. Dark green. Then, in the middle, a standalone island. Dominating the room.

On this island, there are currently rows of trays. Containing food to be cooked. Canapes. Starters. Desserts. Standing in her kitchen and looking over these trays. Imogen thought there was a lot to do.

The glasses had to be polished. The table laid. The staff instructed. Everything had to be just right. They had a reputation to maintain, after all.

Looking out the window over the moor, she thought

about the party. If it would be the last they had. She did not know the details. Anthony had spared her the legal jargon. Thank God. But she knew they had messed up and that it was going to cost them.

She wondered how they would manage if the firm went under. Would they need to sell the house? Downsize? She could not bear the thought. Claytons had been her home for over twenty years. She could not bear to part with it. And how would she explain it to their friends? To the Rotarians. To the Woman's Institute. How could they host them without their home? All its grandeur adds to the event. Yes, she was deeply worried.

Snap out of it, she thought. It will all be fine. We will find a way.

Anyway, she had the party to focus on. Your daughter's 21st birthday is quite an occasion.

Returning to the matter at hand, she thought about her guests. Both Rebecca and Jessica had already arrived, of course. Later this evening, the rest would join them.

There is Archie. Nice boy. It's a bit naive. Still wasting his time on this alcopop dream. Or something like that. So disappointing. The boy has a decent education. He just needs a proper job. Something respectable and decently paid. I do worry for him. It is clear his business will never succeed. Will he just drag it along out of misplaced hope forever? Propping it up while slowly destroying himself? Anthony says I should not be so pessimistic, that I should give the boy a chance. But honestly, how long are we supposed to tolerate his hobby? When will he grow up?

I mean, look at Rebecca. Studying Law at Oxford. On track for a first. Has an internship at a prestigious city firm. And why? Because she was realistic. And she was ambitious. She realized what she could achieve. What would actually work? And she did it. No ifs, no buts. Through hard work, perseverance, and determination. She applied her natural intellect to achieve success. I am not saying Archie could do the same. No. He has a decent mind. But not in the same league as our Rebecca. But if he applied himself, he could achieve something. Something worthy of the family.

Anyway, apparently, he is bringing a friend with him. I cannot remember the name. Something beginning with S. Anyway, I have never met him. It is a man, though. Which is a shame. Seeing him settle down with a nice girl would be good. Oh well.

Moving into the dining room, she surveyed the space. Yes, she thought. That is acceptable. The surfaces are clean. No dust in sight. The carpet has just been vacuumed.

She looked around the room. At the maroon wallpaper. At the landscapes hanging on the walls. At the long mahogany table going down the middle. She remembered so many memories. Christmas lunches. Birthday celebrations. Oh, she could remember Rebecca's 1st birthday as if it was only yesterday. Over the years, they have made so many memories here. Happy memories. As a family. She felt her eyes start to well up. Pull yourself together, she thought. Wiping it away with her hand. You have things to do, she told herself. Moving to leave the room.

Occupying her mind, she thought it would be nice to see Samantha again, her other niece. Since her sister had died. Both she and Anthony had been Jessica's guardians. She thought they had done it well. Helping her get over the grief and come to terms with her new life. But she did feel that perhaps she had neglected Samantha. Her parents had died, too, but she was an adult, and they were older. The younger girl had to take priority. Thinking now, though, she did not think she had ever asked how Samantha was. How was she coping? Well, she could rectify that. She would find time this weekend for the girl. Her husband was coming as well. Richard. Polite young man. A farmer, I think. Or something like that. Perfectly acceptable.

Looking at her watch, she saw that it was four o'clock. Gosh, she thought. The time has gone fast. I best get ready. Quickly, she headed upstairs.

CHAPTER 4

J essica only arrived an hour ago. Currently, she is unpacking her bag and laying her clothes on the bed, ready to hang up in the wardrobe.

I am so excited. She thinks. This weekend is going to be great. The food. The music. The dancing. Seeing everyone. I just can't wait.

I love birthdays. Seeing the delight people have when getting their presents, the joy of celebrating the start of the next stage of their life. And the surprises. Oh, I do love surprises. And who knows? Perhaps Rebecca will get a surprise tonight. One she deserves, haha.

It will be so great to see them all. I mean, seeing Uncle Tony and Aunt Im will be great, of course. But it wouldn't be as fun if it were just them.

Seeing Becky will be nice. Or Rebecca, as it always is now. God. She has become so serious. So stiff. She needs to relax sometimes. Let her hair down. Actually, have some fun. She really is turning into Aunt Im.

Oh, I love Aunt Im. But she is just so stuffy. Always so snobbish, thinking about what is proper. It is like she was born a century too late. As if she would prefer us in corsets, chaperoned while courting with suitors. Despite this, I do love her. She has always been there for me. But I just wish she would lighten up a little. Who knows? She may even enjoy having some fun.

Anyway, Kate is coming as well. She is the person I'm looking forward to most. You see, she is my best friend. Has been since we were small. Oh, the fun we used to have. Talking about boys, trying on makeup and clothes. Sneaking in magazines under Aunt Im's nose. Yes, it was wonderful. We could tell each other anything. Anything at all. Although we have seemed to have drifted apart a bit now. But I guess it's natural. I'm busy at uni with my new friends there. She is busy at her job. Although we are both in London, we are miles apart. Literally and metaphorically. Still, that's why seeing her this weekend is so important. It will be a chance to catch up.

There will also be the boys: Luke. Such a sweet boy. Rather dishy, too. And Daniel. Well, he can be a bit silly. A bit big-headed. But I think he means well. It will be so great to see them all. The old gang is back together. Just like old times.

In truth, I almost thought they would not come. Not after what Becky did. To Kate. To Luke. To Daniel. I do love her, but she is selfish. There is no denying it. She is the most selfish person I have ever met. I mean. Why can't she be more caring? Just a bit? She needs to learn that success isn't everything. There is more to life. Friends. Relationships. Trust. We all have to do things for others sometimes. Things that are right. That we should do. Things which otherwise would make us feel guilty. And rightly so. She just needs to chill out and have some fun. If there's no fun. What's the point in life?

As she finishes laying her clothes, Jessica moves around her bed, collapsing onto the mattress once she reaches the other side. Despite all that, she thinks this weekend will be great. I wish my parents could be here. It was ten years ago now. I can still remember the day. They had gone to London shopping. I was staying with Aunt Im. I was playing in the garden when Aunt Im came to see me. Her eyes were red. Her face was solemn. That was the day my life changed. God. I miss them. But I know they wouldn't want me to dwell. To mourn them for the rest of my life. You have to move on. Live your life. That's what I've learned. I do wish they could be here, though. Both today, especially, and always.

I hope they would have been proud of me. I managed to get into uni. Fashion design BA. I couldn't believe it. It is my dream. I do love my course. It is so interesting. So creative. But I must admit it is the experience I love most. The parties. The clubs. The fun. So, what if I am not studying all the time? You only have one life. You have to live it. Yes. It is nice coming back to Claytons. But not for too long. One weekend of celebration. Thats enough. Then, back to reality. Back to freedom.

It has been so wonderful recently. So blissful these last few months. I have felt so happy. So joyful. So alive. Sometimes, you meet someone who just changes your world. It makes you realize how wonderful it can be.

Closing her eyes. She thinks of the days ahead. The celebration. The joy. The reunions. But also the tensions. The resentments. The secrets.

CHAPTER 5

After a workout at the gym, Daniel just took a shower. Drying with his towel. He is reflecting on his day. A seminar. A few hours of study. Some rugby practice. And now a workout. A day well spent. He thinks.

Looking down, he sees his wet, muscled torso and his strong arms.

He could not understand fat people. How could they not want to improve themselves, to get some muscle? It wasn't that hard. Just do some exercise. Sport. Cardio. You just had to do it. But some people were just weak. Just lazy. They just wouldn't help themselves.

Not like him. He made sure he was in shape. I mean, who

could resist this? Great body. Great prospects. Great looks. I mean, what a catch.

He is strong. He is proactive. He is the best.

He looked at his phone and saw it was 3 p.m. He'd be catching his train in an hour.

The party would be good. Food. Booze. A nice bed. What more did you need? Yes, it would be a good piss-up.

Getting dressed, he thinks about Rebecca. He thinks she has got the nerve to invite him after what she did. I mean, it may have been her mother who sent the invitation. It doesn't matter, really. He doesn't care what she wants. He is going to be there. How else will he give her his surprise?

After what she did. How she humiliated him. Treated him like nothing more than some mutt. Some idiot. No. She doesn't get to say what he can do anymore. He doesn't care what she thinks. She can go to hell.

CHAPTER 6

This is a nightmare. Yes, it's a nightmare! Hopefully, I'll just wake up, and it won't be happening.

Luke is packing for the journey. Absent-mindedly folding his clothes and placing them into his suitcase. He is currently despairing over his problems.

I mean, is there a way I could not go? I could say I was sick. Had the flu? That I could barely leave my bed? Or I could say I have a family emergency. That my parents are ill? Or do I have an urgent assignment to complete?

Thinking these options through, he decided they would not work. He had spoken to his parents and seen Rebecca only yesterday. He could hardly fake a bed-bound illness that appeared that quickly. That would not work. As for the second option, they all knew his parents. They had all grown up together at Dartmoor. They would know if they were ill, so that wouldn't work either. As for the final option, Rebecca was on his course. She would know he was lying. And he had no intention of giving her the satisfaction.

"Shit."

He proclaimed to the world, staring up to the ceiling as if the almighty would take pity on him. As if he would pick him up and drop him far away, away from the commitments he was dreading.

That is it, then. He is going. There is no way he can get out of it. He is off to Claytons.

Sighing. He moves backwards. Slumping into his chair. It is not that he dislikes Claytons; it is far from it. Some of the happiest memories of his childhood were there. Exploring the moor as children. Playing knights and princesses. Then, as teenagers hanging out on the lawn and listening to music. It was just so relaxed. They felt like they did not have a care in the world. I guess that we didn't have any really. Not then. That was before all the exams. Universities. Jobs. The rat race. It was just them. All together. A group of friends just having fun. No pressures. No worries. Just fun.

I look back on those days fondly. That is not to say I am unhappy. I mean, I have achieved what I wanted to. Good A levels. Got into Law at Oxford. I have a bright future ahead of me. At least I did. And things could be much worse. I have good friends. Caring family. Good health. I shouldn't be so self-pitying, really. I know many others have much worse lives than me. It is just this weekend. I really do not want to go.

Why would I? Rebecca is not my friend. She was, I accept that. But after what she did, she is not one anymore. Friends do not treat others like that, as something that can be manipulated to your advantage. That can be tossed aside when it suits you.

It makes me angry, really. Does over ten years of friendship mean nothing to her? Was it really that meaningless? I thought that we got on well. We used to talk and have fun. I thought that we could trust each other and rely on each other. But no. She showed me that was certainly not the case.

I mean, how dare she? How dare she affect my future like this, damage my prospects. My career. And for what? So she can have an edge. So she can be a step ahead. So she can have another bullet point on her CV. Really, it repulses me that she thinks she can treat people like that.

But really, it kind of makes sense. I have never really gotten to know Anthony. He was away a lot when we were children—building his firm in London. But this does create a lot to live up to. Her father built his firm from scratch. It is a tough follow-up act. Then there is Imogen. She is not a bad person, exactly. But I think she is in part responsible for how Rebecca turned out. In her eyes, Rebecca could do no wrong. She was her golden child. Her prodigy. When they were kids, it was obvious. If Rebecca did something wrong, it was never her fault. It could be Kate's or Daniel's. Or Jess's (After a suitable period of mourning had passed). It could even be mine. But never Rebecca's. That sends a powerful message.

It is also the way she is: so focused on position and status, on money. She taught her daughter one crucial lesson: what is important is where you end up, not how you get there. That describes Rebecca in a nutshell. Of course, there is just a personality element to it as well. Rebecca does have a streak of ruthless ambition and pure selfishness going straight through her. I could see that since we were kids. Maybe that should have been a warning sign. Maybe it is my fault? I should never have trusted her.

Calming down, he thinks there are some things to look forward to. Seeing Kate and Jess will be nice. When was the last time I saw them? It must be a year ago, I think. With them both in London and me studying here, we hardly see each other. It will be nice to catch up. Yes, it will be especially nice to see Jess. I have missed her. Daniel is coming as well. I am not sure if that is a good point or a bad one. He is alright, really. He is just a bit of an idiot. It was funny when we were teenagers. But now that we are growing up, it is just annoying. But who knows? Maybe seeing him for just a weekend will be nice—just enough time for it not to become tiring. There will be others there: Rebecca's parents, who are always welcoming, and some of her family. I don't know any of them. Hopefully, they should be nice. Best to focus on the positives. It is inevitable, so there is no point torturing myself. All I can do now is pray for a train strike.

CHAPTER 7

It is a tough one, really. Am I looking forward to the party or dreading it?

Looking out of the window, the scenery flew past. Kate was being pulled both ways. On the one hand, she was really looking forward to seeing Jess. She also looked forward to seeing Luke and even Daniel as well. But Jess was special. They had been so close. In some ways, she felt guilty. She felt that she could have, maybe, made more of an effort to stay in touch. Of course, she was busy with her job at the café. The friends she had made from that. And they were in completely separate parts of the city, distant from one another. That was the thing about London: it is such an enormous metropolis that you tend to stay in your areas. Your territory. She is in Islington, and I am in Wandsworth. We are so close yet so far. And we have such different lives. She is at university with all her student friends. I am working in a café with new friends I have made there.

Even with this, I still think I have been a bit lazy. She has reached out. She has messaged a few times about meeting up. But I have always had an excuse: I am busy with work. I already have something planned. It was not that I deliberately tried to avoid her; it was just always inconvenient. Perhaps I should have tried harder to find a time.

So that is the good side. Now, the bad. Going to the party meant seeing Rebecca again. That is the thing that I am dreading. It is the expectation, really. I have to be there, all smiling. Supportive. Congratulating her on reaching this milestone in her life and wishing her good luck. And I do not know if I can do it. I am not a good liar. I am honest. And honestly, I do not wish Rebecca good luck with anything. Frankly, I would be happier if all her dreams crashed into a heap. And why not? Is that not what she did to me? She ruined my life. Stopped it in its tracks before it had even begun. And why? Because it benefited her. Because she could. She had seen an opportunity, and she took it. She wanted to get ahead. She didn't care that it would hurt me and destroy my future. She only cared about herself.

But then, what is new? Even as children, she was selfish. Just small things. Taking the last slice of pizza. Taking your makeup. Copying you at school if she needs to. All without asking. But it all shows who she is. She is treacherous. A leech. A snake. She gets what she wants from you and then leaves you—drained of anything she could take.

Sometimes, I wonder why I even became friends with her if her nature was always so obvious. Well, maybe it wasn't. As I said, they were just small things. And we were children. You do not notice it so much back then. You're more innocent. More naïve. And I guess there is Jess as well. We just clicked, and Rebecca was her cousin. By befriending one, you also got the other. Oh well. How could you tell that a childhood friendship would end up meaning nothing? Not in the face of relentless ambition and self-interest. All those days at school. Evenings under the stars. Afternoons lazy on the lawn. All that time, you thought something existed. Something that had worth. When actually, on their side, there was obviously nothing at all. No friendship. No loyalty. Nothing.

Seeing green fields and rolling hills come into view. With sheep only appearing as white dots. Only there for a moment. Then pulled away. She thought about her other problem. Imogen. She had no problem with the woman herself. On the contrary, she had always been nice to her. She was always very accommodating when she came around or stayed at Clayton's. But seeing her and Tony would be difficult. It would be uncomfortable. What if she knew? What if she found out? She didn't want to hurt her. Or want to be hurt by her. It was all a mess. It's all far too close to home. What had she been thinking? Well, she knew the answer to that. Nothing. It had been a whirlwind. A bit of fun. She just got caught up in the moment. Flew away with her heart. But her head was in control now. It knew that this was bad. It was dangerous. How could she hide it? Make sure she did not suspect anything. For the whole weekend? God, it was going to be terrible. Always second-guessing her every move and always having something to hide.

Looking at the overhead display, she saw she was not far from her stop now. Here it goes. She thought. No turning back now.

CHAPTER 8

The lounge at Clayton's is perhaps what you would expect: oak-panelled walls hanging beautiful art, mostly scenes of the sea. Waves crashing, creating beautiful shades of white and blue, with a few oil portraits hanging as well. The skill shown in them is quite remarkable. At the centre of the back wall is a white marble fireplace, the mantelpiece lined with bronze ornaments—a silver clock at the centre. Facing the fire is a red leather sofa. Old-fashioned but still stylish and comfortable. On either side are two armchairs of the same design. Together, they surround the fire, creating a natural seating area.

Tony is sitting in one of the armchairs, with thick, styled silver hair and smooth, unwrinkled skin. He is doing well for a man in his early fifties. Of course, you never know how much help he has, although he does help himself. He is the type of man who radiates easy confidence. He has a certain charm and smoothness that comes naturally to him. He is someone comfortable in any situation. Whether or not he is being genuine as well is another matter.

Reading through his Times, Tony is enjoying his moment of relaxation. He is looking forward to the party, but he is enjoying having some peace and quiet before they all arrive. He only returned from London yesterday, straight from work. So, he knows he should savour it while he can. Once all the guests arrive, he will become the host. Well, deputy host, really. Imogen always takes the reins, something that Tony is rather glad about.

Imogen is sitting on the corner of the sofa closest to him. She is sitting, completing the crossword. It has been their tradition for over ten years. He gets the Times and gives her the crossword. The secret to a successful marriage, really. Finding your way. Your routine. Together.

At just that moment, Jessica strolls into the room, grinning. She flops against the back of the sofa, leaning over and kissing Imogen on the cheek.

"Hi."
She says in a high-pitched squeal.
"Hello dear," Imogen replies.
"Yes, hello, Jessica."
Tony adds. Oh well, He thinks. The peace was good while it lasted.

Imogen puts her crossword on the side table. Jessica

comes round and sits in the other corner of the sofa, falling into it and looking sprawled as if it were absorbing her whole.

"When is everyone else arriving?"

Jessica asks.

"In the early evening."

Imogen replied.

"They all said they would be here by seven o'clock."

"Oh, wonderful. It will be so nice to see everyone again. Are they all coming?"

"Yes. Luke, Daniel, Kate, Samantha, Richard, and Archie. They are all coming."

"Brilliant. Is Archie coming with anyone?"

"Yes, as a matter of fact. Some friend of his, unfortunately. Why can't the boy not just find some nice girl? I really do not know."

"Oh, don't be so prudish, Aunt Im. He is young. He has every right to be free and single. We don't all want to tie ourselves down just yet."

Imogen caught Jessica's eye.

"So, there is no one that you are going out with? You are not tied down yourself yet?"

She asked.

Jessica looked away.

"Well, I mean."

She said, blushing.

"I have met people in London. I will just see what happens, I guess. Anyway, what about Rebecca? The last I heard, she does not have anyone?"

"Oh, she is far too busy. Studying law is demanding, you know. There are so many exams and such a lot to cover. No, she is rightly focusing on her career. Isn't that right, Anthony?"

He looked up from his paper.

"Well, it is challenging, yes. Although I still think it is possible to have some fun as well."

"I agree."

Said Jessica.

"She is far too serious. She needs to let her hair down a bit. Relax. There is more to life than work."

Imogen fixed her with a serious gaze.

"Relaxing does not get you into Oxford, nor will it get you a successful legal career. There is nothing wrong with being ambitious and hard-working."

Jessica rolled her eyes.

"Well, she can relax on her birthday, at least!"

She said.

Imogen smiled, her face softening.

"Yes."

She said fondly.

"Yes, she can."

"So."

Imogen said brightly,

"How is your course going? Are your studies going well?"

"Yes. I love it."

Jessica exclaimed.

"I love learning about all these designs and styles and being inspired. Thinking about what I want to do."

"Good dear. I am glad to hear that you are working hard."

"Yeah…"

Jessica replied with a slight lingering. Her discomfort is subtly showing.

"So, Uncle Tony."

Changing the subject. She asks.

"How is the firm doing?"

He looked up from his paper again.

"Yes."

He smiled; his flawless teeth were on full display.

"It is going well. It's normal, really. Lots to do. I won't bore you with the details."

His eyes shifted momentarily to his wife. Their eyes locked, and her face was fixed in a smile. Both of them were complicit in the lies he had just told.

"By the way."

He said absently, subtly changing the subject.

"Darling, how are the preparations going?"

He asked, smoothly directing everyone's focus to a new topic.

Imogen sighed.

"Well, it all seems to be going well so far. I have checked, and the cleaning is up to standard. The caterer dropped off some of the food earlier and will return soon the rest of their staff. All the rooms are made up and ready for the guests. So yes, it is all going to plan. It is just that there is always the worry that something will happen. That something will go wrong."

"Nonsense."

Richard replied.

"You are doing splendidly. With you in charge, how could anything possibly go wrong? I do not think they would dare."

He joked, directing a small smile toward Jessica.

Coming through the door, Rebecca appeared. Tall and

slim with dark hair. She towered over the rest of them. Jessica leaped up.

"Hello Becky"

Jessica screamed, devouring Rebecca in a hug and taking the woman quite by surprise.

"Sorry, Rebecca. How are you? How is Oxford?"

"Yes"

Rebecca made a slight smile.

"It is good, thank you. All very busy."

She said this with a slightly superior tone as if Jessica were a child who needed occupying.

"And how is yours?"

She asked.

"All of that sewing must be very peaceful."

"Well, there is a bit more to it than that. I mean, we learn about different fashion houses and schools of thought. But yes, there is sewing."

Just then, a car could be heard pulling up on the gravel drive. Jessica rushed to the window.

"Oh god."

She yelled.

"It's Kate. She's here."

She ran out of the room, with Imogen slowly rising and following.

"You should not do that, you know."

Tony said, looking at Rebecca.

"Learning fashion design is a worthwhile thing to do."

"Oh, come on, Dad. I mean, she might as well go and work in a sweatshop in Bangalore. It is hardly a proper degree, is it."

He sighed.

"Darling. People do different things. Just because she has gone down a different path, it does not make it any less valuable than yours."

She rolled her eyes.

"Okay, Dad. If you say so."

CHAPTER 9

Coming up to Claytons again, Kate felt a mix of emotions: happiness that her journey had finished. Excitement that she would see Jess again. Disgust that she would see Rebecca again. And nervous that she would see Imogen again.

The car pulled up, and she opened the door to get out. Suddenly, she heard someone running. Then, in a flash, Jessica burst through the doorway and jumped on her, smothering her in a hug.

"Kate."
She yelled.
"You are here. Oh, I have missed you."
Kate smiled. Well, Jess hadn't changed then. She put her arms around Jess and squeezed.
"Yes, Jess, I have missed you too."

"Well, I see you two have been reunited."

Said Imogen, coming through the doorway. Jessica and Kate let go of each other.

"How are you, dear? I hope you had a pleasant journey?"

Said Imogen. She came out and kissed Kate on the cheek.

"Yes."

Kate said, feeling slightly flustered.

"It was great, thank you."

Immediately, she thought that she had come on a bit strong. She had come from a train from London to Exeter, not the Orient Express. Seeing Imogen again after so long made her feel guilty. Here was a woman who had always been kind to her, yet she betrayed her.

"Good. Good. Well, I will leave you two to get reacquainted."

Imogen said, walking back inside.

Jessica turned to Kate. A huge grin spread across her face. She put her arm through Kate's.

"Why don't we go for a walk? Then I can find out all the trouble you have been getting into?"

"Yes, that would be wonderful."

Kate replied cheerfully. You do not know the half of it. She thought.

They walked to the left, off the gravel drive and onto the grounds, the freshly cut grass beneath them.

"So, how have you been?"

Jessica asked.

"Yes, I have been good but busy. There are always shifts going at work. And then there's clubbing and parties. It never really stops, does it."

Jessica laughed.

"No, not really. But would you want it to?"

"God, no."

They both shared a giggle.

"And how are you? How is Uni going? Are you on your way to making the next Gucci?"

"Oh, it is brilliant. It is just so interesting. We learn about all these different ideas and techniques. It is just so inspiring, you know. It just makes you want to get out there and do it for yourself."

"Well, why don't you?"

"Oh, I will. But there is just so much more left to learn. I just cannot wait. And there is the fun: so many clubs, parties, drinks. It does make you realize how little there is here."

Jessica said, looking around at the wilderness that surrounded them.

"Yes."

Kate agreed.

"It does put things into perspective. When we were younger, it seemed like heaven. But now, I do not think I could ever live here."

"Exactly. I mean, do not get me wrong; I do love it. I loved growing up here hanging out with you. It was great. But now I have experienced London. It just has so much more to offer. I will always visit here. But I could never live here. I would get bored to death. Or turn into a clone of Aunt Im. Not sure which is worse."

Kate hit Jess's shoulder with a playful slap.

"Stop it. Your aunt is lovely. Just a bit…"

"Victorian?"

"I was going to say traditional."

"I know. I do love her. I just wish she would relax some-times. I do worry that she is so concerned about how things look that it makes her unhappy. And it feels like Becky is just the same."

Kate tensed slightly, tightening her grip around Jessica's arm.

"Sorry."

Jessica blurted out.

"I did not think. I am sorry."

They were silent for a moment.

"To tell you the truth, I almost thought you would not come."

Jessica said.

"I thought you would not want to be here."

Kate turned to her. She sighed.

"Well, that is partly true. I do not want to be here to see Rebecca. I would happily never see her again. But I do want to be here as well. To see you. It seems like we would never be able to otherwise."

Jessica turned and gripped her in a hug.

"I am so sorry for what she did to you. I still cannot believe she did it. I should have done something, said some-thing. I was just afraid. A coward. Aunt Im would never have believed me."

"Hey. Look at me."

As Jessica raised her head, Kate could see her eyes welling up.

"You are not responsible for what happened. Okay. The

only person who is responsible is her. It is her fault."

Jessica nodded, easing her grip. She wiped her face.

"Have you spoken to her since it happened?"

"No."

Kate replied.

"She did not reach out to me, so I certainly did not want to chase after her."

Jessica nodded.

"It still baffles me."

She went on.

"That she would do that. That she could do that. We had been friends since we were ten. And she still did it. She still ruined my future. My life."

"Hey. Your life is not ruined. I mean, look at you. You are gorgeous. You are young. Healthy. I mean, sure, working in a café is not what you wanted. But you have made it work. You have made new friends. You have built a new life. You are amazing."

Kate looked at her friend. God. She had missed her.

"Well, yes"

She admitted.

"I am amazing."

"There you go. Who knows? Maybe someone will switch Becky's gin and tonic for some white vinegar."

Kate turned sharply. Jessica struggled to hide a smile. It became infectious, and they both broke out into laughter.

"Jess."

Kate yelled.

"I was only joking. If I did that, especially today, Aunt Im would kill me. I do not love you that much. Not enough to do that. But do you remember the old days?

"Oh yes. You were awful."

"No, I wasn't. I just did a few tricks: switched the salt and sugar, put cling film on the toilet seat."

"Putting ten Mentos into Daniel's bottle of Coke,"

Kate interrupted.

"Oh god. That was hilarious. I don't think he spoke to me for a week after that."

They both broke into laughter.

Jessica put her hand on Kate's wrist.

"It is so great to see you. We should do it more often."

"Yes, we should. I am sorry that I have not made much of an effort to since we left."

"Do not be silly. We were both busy. It just happens. And we are here now, aren't we?"

Yes, thought Kate, that we are. Whether or not that would be for the best, she was still not sure.

CHAPTER 10

"So, how bad is it?" Rebecca asked.

Tony raised his head from reading the paper. "How bad is what?"

He replied.

Imogen, now returned to her crossword, was also engaged.

"Do not treat me like an idiot, Dad. The firm. How bad is it?"

How did she know about that? Imogen thought. She had not told her. Her father clearly hadn't. Perhaps rumours had begun to spread. Yes, that seemed likely. She was a law student, after all. Oh God. It really does make it all real.

Tony paused for a moment before sighing, folding up his paper, and placing it on the side. He then turned to face Rebecca.

"It is bad, darling."

He said.

"How bad?"

She asked.

"Really bad."

"What has happened?"

Tony waved his arm dismissively.

"It does not matter."

"Tell me!"

Rebecca demanded. The way he was acting, as if this was not important, was starting to frustrate her.

"Fine. There was a case at work. A dispute in a hostile takeover. We used some methods that we thought would win the case. But it backfired. The opposition found out. They presented evidence of these methods to the judge. He ruled in their favour. And now the client is suing us for malpractice."

As he said this, his face grew tense. For once, it almost appeared that he was uncomfortable.

"Methods? What methods?"

"What the methods were is not important. What is important is the firm is in trouble. Frankly, it could go under."

Go under! Anthony had said there were problems. He said that a client was suing them for malpractice, but he never said he thought they could go under before. Hearing the words made a mass of thoughts come into Imogen's mind. The house? Rebecca? Jessica? Their marriage? How would it all cope? The firm was their livelihood. It was what had provided all this. Without it, they would have nothing. No income. The thought terrified her.

Then, her mind drifted to these methods. Well, she loved Anthony. But she knew who she had married. He was a skilled lawyer. A great one. But she knew that, if necessary, he would use underhanded tactics. He would do everything he could to win. So, what had he done this time? Broken the law? And what would this mean? Could he be prosecuted? Disbarred? Oh, the shame. The humiliation. How could he have been so stupid? To risk everything that they had built for a single case? Well, she knew how. His ego. Anthony hated to lose.

"Surely one malpractice case would not bankrupt the firm."

Rebecca said, bringing Imogen back to the present.

"Surely you can make a settlement."

"It is not quite as simple as that."

Tony said, his irritation was clearly showing.

"Even if they would settle out of court, the reputational damage has already been done. Word has begun to spread that we made a mistake. That we are being sued by a client. Our other clients are losing confidence. They are leaving. That is the real danger. That by the time we get to court, we will have no clients left."

They all sat there, silent for a moment. Stunned. Everything was going wrong.

"But what does that mean for us?"

Rebecca asked.

"For our family? How will it affect us?"

Tony put his head in his hands, surprising the others. Rebecca did not think she had ever seen her father like this. He was always composed, prepared, and comfortable with whatever was thrown at him. Clearly, this whole affair had shaken him more than he showed.

He raised his head. He looked exhausted. Drained. Exhaling deeply, he said.

"To be honest, darling, I do not know. The firm is our main source of income. Without it, we cannot afford all this."

He said, gesturing around him.

"It might be the case that we would have to sell the house."

Imogen flinched.

"Buy a smaller property."

Tony continued.

"And use the remainder to live off. We may have no choice."

Again, they were all silent.

"I cannot believe it."

Rebecca said.

Her father nodded in agreement.

"I cannot believe you have done this to me!"

She screamed.

Tony raised his head to look at her.

"Excuse me?"

He asked.

"My inheritance. My future. You have put it all at risk. How could you? How dare you?"

"How dare I? Darling, you need to calm down. Yes, I made a mistake. I admit that. But your future is not threatened.

Once you have your degree. At first, I have no doubt. You will have endless opportunities."

"That firm was my inheritance. My birthright. I should have taken it once you retired. And now it is gone. Just like that. All because you were stupid enough to break the law. Do not bother denying it. It is obvious."

"Rebecca."

Tony said, his voice hardening and his anger coming through.

"What that firm was is over thirty years of my hard work. My drive. My sacrifice. From it, we provided you with everything you could ever need. We ensured you had the best. So do not accuse me of ruining your life. Without my work, you would have had nothing!"

"Well, Dad, you need not have bothered. I now have nothing anyway!"

Tony was silent, his face fixed in a scowl. His eyes focused on his daughter. The ungrateful brat, he thought. After everything I have done for her. Not even an ounce of respect. Not one word of understanding. Of support. No. She just thinks about herself. Not even her mother. Just about what she thinks she will lose. How dare she.

Before he could reply, Rebecca turned and stormed out of the room. Both he and Imogen looked at each other. They both had the same thought: What are we going to do?

As Rebecca came out into the hall, Jessica and Kate came in through the front door. As they saw each other, there was a moment of stillness. They were both hesitant.

Rebecca was the first to move. She casually walked over and said.

"Kate, how lovely to see you. Have you had a nice journey?"

She came in and kissed Kate on the cheek. Kate did not move; her body was tense. She did not return the greeting.

Her face tightened into a slight smile. Just enough to be polite, Kate said.

"Yes, thank you. The journey was pleasant."

Her voice was heavy as if every civil word she spoke was a chore.

"Excellent. I was so glad to hear you could make it. Thank God you have gotten over all that unpleasantness."

Jessica stared. She could not believe Rebecca had just said that. That she has the nerve. God. Rebecca could be impossible. She just could not resist.

After a moment, Kate said.

"That unpleasantness? I think you mean the destruction of my career before it had even begun, which you caused."

She was feeling hot, the rage boiling inside her, struggling to maintain her act of calmness.

"Which I caused? Darling, I think you will find it was your actions that were responsible. I only did what any honest person should do. Must do. It pained me to do it. But standards must be maintained. In the end, it will be good for you."

Good? Kate thought. Did she just say that it would be good for me? God. After what she did, she has the nerve to blame me. To stand there. As bold as brass. To act as if she did not lie. That she did not use me, betray me. And to say that, it pained her. Wow. She really is a piece of work.

As the rage. The resentment. Builds up within her. Threatening to boil over. She suddenly feels a light touch on her wrist. She peers down and sees Jess's hand. The feeling brings her some reassurance. I am not alone. I am not the only one who knows what she did.

Putting her hand in Jess's, she calms. You must be calm, she tells herself, for Jess.

Kate smiles.
"Well, I guess we will have to agree to disagree."
She says. It is taking every ounce of her restraint not to strangle the woman.
"Well, tell yourself whatever you wish."
Replies Rebecca with a sly smile.
"See you later."
She says, making her way toward the stairs and up.
Once she is gone, Jessica bursts.
"I am so sorry. I cannot believe she did that—the nerve. And I am so sorry I did not say something. I just froze. I felt like I was paralyzed, just watching."
"It is ok."
Says Kate.
"I know it is difficult. She is your cousin."
"But it is not ok."

Jessica protests.

"That she has gotten away with it. What she has done to you. She should not be able to do that."

"Yes, She shouldn't."

Kate agrees, seeing her friend upset. She puts on a brave face.

"Cheer up."

She says, looping their arms back together.

"We have the party later. We can drink enough to forget all about her."

Jessica smiles, and they both laugh.

CHAPTER II

Archie was right about one thing, Sebastien thought. The scenery is quite stunning—the wild grass, with large mounds dotted across, as if they have burst through the ground. Lawns of gorse bushes make up the moorland. Giant crags of rock dominate the landscape. Yes, it did have a certain beauty—a wild, uncontrollable kind.

He was now with Archie in a taxi, travelling through roads on the moor and seeing these views from his window. Their destination was the house of Archie's uncle.

"So, I am guessing you packed a dinner jacket?"
Archie cut in.
Dinner jacket? I thought. Oh no.
"No, I have not."
I replied.
"Why?"

"Well, it is just that the party is black tie; that is all. I assumed you knew."

Oh, brilliant.

"What? Why would I know that? Am I some telepath now? Am I able to read your mind to instinctively know the dress code? God Archie. What am I going to do? I just packed a striped shirt. I am going to look like a complete idiot."

"Well, at least you will give them an accurate impression."

Archie replied, laughing.

I frowned.

"This is not funny. I am going to arrive at a house full of strangers and be underdressed. In fact, it would be better to arrive dressed in nothing at all. At least then, I could blame it on a psychotic breakdown. For goodness' sake, Archie. Why didn't you tell me?"

"Calm down, I am only joking."

Archie said joyfully, getting his breath back after nearly falling off his seat after the breakdown comment.

Sebastien breathed.

"Oh, thank God. So it is not black tie?"

"Oh no, it is black tie…"

Archie confirmed.

"What?"

I interrupted.

"What do you mean? If it is black tie, then how are you joking? What are you on about?"

"Easy. It is black tie, but you have got nothing to worry about. I packed a dinner jacket for you. There. Happy?"

"You packed me a suit?"

I asked. Puzzled.

"How? You do not know my size?"

"I asked Kiera. She found one for me that would fit."
"Kiera? How did she know?"
I asked. Completely confused.
Archie sighed.
"Seb. Come on. She works in a clothes shop, for goodness sake. Of course, she knows your measurements. She could tell them from a mile off."
"She knows my measurements. What? Even my inside leg?"
"Yes. Even that. I did wonder about that, you know."
Archie remarked, a small smirk emerging.
"What do you mean, 'you wondered'?"
I said defensively.
"Well, it is an interesting area for a person to be familiar with. Did make me wonder."

Archie turned to me and made a librarian-like look. His face tilted down, his eyes looking up at me.

"Oh, do not be ridiculous."
I replied, starting to blush.
"Well, I was only curious."
Archie said smugly.
"Ridiculous."
I repeated, turning back to the window.
"Look."
Archie said, pointing forward.
"We are getting close now."

Following his gaze, I could see a large stone building in the distance.

"How long has your uncle had the place?"

I asked.

"Oh, forever, really. They have always lived at Claytons. For as long as I can remember, anyway. They have had it all the time Rebecca has been alive. I can remember that. So that must be twenty-one years at least."

"Big place."

I commented.

"What do they do, your aunt and uncle?"

"Well, Aunt Imogen does not work. Has not done so for decades, at least. And Uncle Tony? He works in law. Corporate, I think. A type that is very lucrative anyway."

"I see. But surely, he does not do his legal work all the way out here?"

"No. He has a flat in the city. He stays there in the week and comes back at the weekends."

"Really?"

I asked. Surprised.

"Surely it would be easier. It would make more sense if they just moved to London?"

Archie thought for a moment.

"Yes. I guess you are right, really. I never really thought about it before. But Aunt Imogen does love it here. I suspect she will never leave."

I shrugged, cocking my head to one side. Our roots. Once you have put them down, let them grow. It can be tough pulling them back up.

Coming closer to the house now. I could see it in more detail.

It was a large building. Greystone. Perhaps granite. It was built in a traditional style. Natural rocks are kept in their original shapes and held together with cement. It had two storeys. Four sets of windows. Looking out the front. With a view of the moor. On both floors. A slate roof over the top. Leading up to the front of the house was a gravel drive. Where there was a set of three stone steps leading to the door. A large oak door painted black. A golden knocker at its centre.

Exiting the car, I looked around at the scenery. The rough terrain. The craggy rocks. Although the house was beautiful and completely comfortable, I was sure. Its location did create a certain feeling of remoteness. That you were completely alone, I was sure it would be pleasant enough to visit. But to live here. No. I felt that, over time, it would drive me mad.

Turning to the door, I saw a middle-aged man and woman come out. These I presumed to be Archie's aunt and uncle.

"Archie."
The woman said. Smiling. She embraced him. Kissing him on the cheek.
"Lovely to see you."
"Hello. Aunt Imogen."
Archie replied uncomfortably. He put his hand out towards the man.
"Uncle Tony."

Tony reached out and took the hand.

"Archie."

He said with a flawless smile.

"It is great you could make it."

Looking at him, I could see what Archie meant. Smooth was certainly the word. I could certainly see him charming captains of industry, negotiating their contracts and justifying his fees.

He turned to me, appraising me.

"Aren't you going to introduce us to your friend?"

"Yes, of course. Uncle Tony, Aunt Imogen, this is my friend Sebastien."

Archie said proudly, gesturing to me.

"Pleasure to meet you."

Said Imogen, tight-lipped with a thin smile, presenting a hand. Her previous gesture was clearly reserved for more familiar guests.

"Likewise,"

I said. Taking her hand.

"Tony"

Tony said, leaning forward with his hand outstretched.

"It was good of you to come."

His large smile was still firmly in place.

I took his hand.

"Thank you for having me."

I said.

"Not a problem."

Tony replied.

"A friend of Archie's is a friend of ours."

Imogen did not appear quite so convinced.

"So."

She asked.

"What made you decide to join Archie on his trip?"

"He has always wanted to see Dartmoor."

Archie cut in before I could respond.

"It seemed like an excellent opportunity."

They turned to me, and Archie widened his eyes. In the universal signal of 'Just go along with it.'

"Yes."

I said, smiling.

"It has always been somewhere I have wanted to visit. Archie told me about your party and said I should come."

Not wanting to appear to have muscled in.

"Yes, well. It is a wonderful place. We have always loved it. Haven't we, darling?"

Tony replied, turning to his wife.

"Yes, It is beautiful."

She agreed, turning to the scenery.

"We are truly blessed to live here."

At just that moment, they could hear another car coming down the driveway.

Once the taxi stopped, a man and a woman, both in their early thirties, stepped out with their bags.

She was of average height, with dark hair and a healthy build. He was taller, with brown hair and a slightly athletic frame. Clearly, they were a couple.

"Samantha."

Imogen cried.

"It is wonderful to see you. How are you?"

Rushing to her, she embraced her with a kiss on the cheek.

"Hi, Aunty."
She replied.
"Yes, we are great, thank you. The journey was uneventful,
fortunately.
Smiling. Imogen turned to the man.
"Richard. Handsome as ever. Are you well?"
She asked, kissing him on the cheek.

Yep. It was clear I was the only stranger at this weekend.
Maybe I should drag Archie to my cousin's wedding next
month? Yes, that was a pleasant thought.

Tony turned to them both. He said the usual greetings,
kissing Samantha and shaking Richard's hand. His smile was
still plastered on his face.

Once Archie had done the same, they all turned to me.

"And who is this?"
Samantha asked, sizing me up.
"This is Sebastien."
Archie said.
"He is a friend of mine, joining me for this weekend."
I put out my hand.
"Lovely to meet you."
I said. She grabbed my arm, hugged me and kissed me on
the cheek.

"Yes. It is lovely to meet you as well."
She said.
Putting out his hand, Richard said.
"Pleasure."
We shook.
"Right."
Imogen cut in.
"I think we should go in, shall we? It is getting rather chilly
out here."

With us all nodding in agreement, we made our way to the
door.

We naturally formed a kind of column: Imogen and Tony
at the front, Richard and Archie in the middle, and Samantha
and I at the back.

"So."
She said as we climbed up the steps.
"What brings you to Claytons, then?"
She asked, intrigued.
"I have always wanted to come to Dartmoor."
I said.
"Archie mentioned he was visiting and said I should tag
along."
"That's nice. It is such a beautiful place."
"Yes, it is. So, where are you from?"
"London. I work at St. Thomas's."
"The hospital? Are you a medic?"
"A nurse, yes. I have been for over ten years now. I started
training when I left school."

"And you enjoy it? And do you like living in London?"

"Yes. I still love it as much as I did when I first started. I mean, it is not always easy. We are always understaffed. But I do it because it is who I am. I could never imagine doing anything else. And yes, I love living in London. It does cost a fortune, but there is nowhere else like it, with so much to see and do."

"Samantha."

Imogen cut in.

"Could you show Sebastien to the green room? It is where he will be staying."

"Of course,"

Turning her attention to me, Samantha said.

"Come on, it is up here."

Gesturing to the stairs.

We made our way up.

"It is lucky I work at St Thomas's."

She said.

"Otherwise, I may never have met Richard—just a normal day. I am doing my rounds, and bang, we bump into each other. The luckiest moment of my life."

A huge smile grew on her face.

"How long have you been together?"

I asked, pleased that the woman had found a husband she clearly adored.

"Oh, for eight years now. It has been wonderful. It is, isn't it? When you find that person. The one you truly love, who truly understands you."

"Yes. I can imagine."

"Ah. We are here," She says. Indicating a green wooden door.

"The green room?"
I asked, pointing to the door.
"Yes. The green room. Not just the door, either."
She joked.
"I will leave you to get ready. It was lovely chatting with you.
"Yes, and you."
I replied.

She turned and walked away. Watching her go, I thought what a pleasant woman she was. Confident and friendly. Hopefully, they were all like her. Well, perhaps that was too much to hope for.

After a moment, I turned to enter my room. All I could think about now was getting in the shower.

CHAPTER 12

It was quite nice being back, I had to admit, Archie thought as he walked down the corridor. The house. The scenery. It all reminded me of my childhood. Every summer, my family would come down here to visit Uncle Tony and the rest. It was fun. Running around on the moor and climbing up the rocks and feeling like you were scaling Everest. Oh, childhood. Everything was so much simpler then. No stress. No commitments. Back then, I did not have to make polite small talk with my family. I could just run off onto the moor. Have an adventure. Back then, that was considered cute. Now, it would be considered rude. Ah well. It was great while it lasted.

Having washed and changed, Archie was now walking down the corridor to Sebastien's room. I do not think it was too bad. He thought. I mean, Aunt Imogen was a bit frosty towards Seb. But what should I have expected? I did warn him about her. Uncle Tony was very welcoming, of course—good old Uncle Tony. You can always rely on him to lend a helping hand. Seb and Samantha seemed to get on well with each other. They were chatting about something or other as they climbed the stairs. Yes. I think this will go rather well.

As he turned a corner, He started to hear voices: a woman and a man. As he got closer, he could clearly identify the female voice as Rebecca's. He did not know the male voice, though. What he could tell, though, was that it was not a friendly discussion. Their voices were raised. The hostility was clear. It was clearly a confrontation.

"Seriously? Do you really not accept that you did anything wrong?"
The man said.

Both feeling slightly awkward but also intrigued, Archie slowed and stopped by the door, listening in.

"No. I seriously do not accept that I did anything wrong, Luke. It was an honest mistake."
"An honest mistake?"
Luke said sarcastically.
"Pull the other one, Rebecca. There was nothing honest about it. You deliberately did it on purpose. You deliberately misled me.
He said angrily.
"Mislead you? Luke, I think you are getting a bit paranoid."

She replied in a slightly patronizing tone.

"They made a mistake. That is all. That does not mean I was responsible for what happened. That does not mean that it was my fault you did not get it."

"Don't!"

He shouted.

"Do not do that. You know it was your fault. You know what they are like. No. You did this intentionally. You lied to me. You deliberately misled me. All so you could take it."

He paused, taking a large breath. I suspect he was overcome with emotion.

"Did it really mean that little?"

He asked.

"Our childhood? Our friendship? Over ten years of trust? Of loyalty? Was it really worth so little? Such a small price to pay for your success? We were friends, Rebecca. And you betrayed me. Betrayed us. What you did to Kate. And to Daniel as well. You just threw us all under the bus. You just used us. Tossed us away once you got what you wanted. Like we were nothing. Worthless. It was disgusting. How could you do it?"

For a minute or so, there was silence. I could feel the tension from out here.

"Ok, seeing as you are finished."

Rebecca said calmly.

"I will say this: you clearly have decided to paint me as the villain. You have decided that I am responsible for your failure and for that of Kate and Daniel. To pin it all on me.

But that is just not true. The truth is you are all responsible for your actions. Your failures. Perhaps one day you will come to understand that. To accept responsibility. Once you have calmed down, I think you will see this. And we can move on."

There was another pause. The tension remained.

"Huh"

Luke grunted finally, rather dismissively.

"I see… I see that you are unbelievable. You will never admit it, will you? Never admit to what you have done. To the sins you have committed to ensure your success. You know, I really am disappointed. I thought you might have some remorse. That in hindsight, you might have realized how much you hurt us. How much pain you caused? But no. Now, I do not think you will ever change." He paused for another moment. "God help you, Rebecca. In the end, our sins have a way of coming back on us. Of giving us what we deserve."

Just after this, Archie heard footsteps. Heavy and fast coming towards the door. Quickly, he ran backwards, making an effort to move quietly, stepping on the tips of his toes, and hid back around the corner.

Out of the room came a young, athletic man. As soon as he appeared, he turned quickly and went in the opposite direction. Towards the stairs.

Archie let out a sigh of relief. God. That was horrible. The atmosphere in there was enough to make him feel physically sick. But he was intrigued. What had Rebecca done? If she had done anything at all? As she rejected Luke's accusations. And why did Luke blame her so passionately? What was it that he had lost? What was it that Rebecca had done to Kate and Daniel? Who even were Kate and Daniel?

So many questions. Archie wondered if he would ever find out the answers.

CHAPTER 13

Unpacking his clothes in his bedroom, Sebastien could see what Samantha meant. The walls and ceiling of his room were all dark green. The side walls were wood-panelled, whereas those to his front and back were plastered. But they were both painted the same colour. It was not unattractive, really. Just very, well, green. But it could have been worse. The carpet was soft. The mattress is comfortable—the pillows are light. And the bathroom was clean. If nothing else, he would sleep well.

Against the back wall, next to the door, a four-poster mahogany bed had been placed, with a bedside table on each side. Against the left wall was a large wardrobe made of the same wood. On the right was a door that led to the bathroom. And on the front wall, a window looked over the gravel drive and onto the moor. In the left corner, a high-backed chair stood.

All in all, it was actually quite nice. He had stayed in far worse places. Maybe it would not be so bad after all.

Just then, he heard a knock at his door.

"Can I come in?"
He heard Archie ask.
"If you must."
He replied jokingly.

The door opened, and Archie stepped inside.

"So how are you finding your lodgings then? Not too basic for you, is it?"
He teased.
"I will admit it. It is nice. Although it is a bit green, it is a nice colour. There is just so much of it."
Archie looked around the room.
"Yes, there is, isn't there? Oh well, it could be worse. It could be bright pink."
Sebastien chuckled.
"Yes. I suppose that is true. So, how are you settling in? Just like old times?"
"Oh. Yes. It is fine. To be honest, I have barely been here since I was a kid. Back then, it was all so exciting. Going onto the wild moors for an adventure. Now, the greatest adventure I will get is trying to avoid Aunt Imogen."
"Do not say that. She seems nice."
"Oh, come on. She hardly gave you the welcome party. She

is pleasant enough. It is because she is just so judgemental. I can almost feel her disapproval of me."

"Come now. She seemed happy to see you and must like you enough to invite you. Perhaps you should give her the benefit of the doubt. It may help you enjoy your time here."

Sebastien suggested.

"I guess."

Replied Archie reluctantly.

"Speaking of my relatives, you will never believe what I just heard about Rebecca?"

"I mean. We are in a house full of your relatives. So, it is quite likely that we were going to speak of them at some point."

"Do you want to hear about the argument or not?"

Sebastien was curious.

"Sorry. Go on."

"As I was saying."

Said Archie. Coming over and sitting on the bed.

"I just heard Rebecca have a great big row with someone called Luke. I am guessing he is one of her friends. Well, not anymore, apparently. He certainly is not related to me. Anyway, He was going on about how she betrayed him. Mislead him. Lied to him. He was furious. And she just denied it. She said he was blaming his failings all on her. That his actions were his responsibility, and he should accept it."

Sebastien was listening intently, his hands together. His eyes were focusing on them in thought.

"Interesting"

He murmured.

"What happened next?"

"Well,"

Archie continued.

"He said that she was unbelievable, that he thought that in hindsight she might regret it, but she clearly hadn't."

He paused.

"He also said that our sins have a way of catching up with us."

Sebastien turned to him.

"Do you mean, like, a threat?"

He asked, concerned.

"I am not sure."

Archie replied.

"He did not sound menacing. He had calmed down a bit, but there was still a feeling in his voice. I only heard them through the door, so I cannot say."

Sebastien nodded. "Well, he is right. From a psychological standpoint, at least. Our past sins have a way of coming back to us in the present. Of causing us harm."

"I am not sure that will be a problem with Rebecca. As I said, she is ruthless. I do not think she would care as long as she achieved what she wanted. However, I cannot be certain that he was right. But it would not surprise me."

"Do you have any idea what he could be referring to?"

Sebastien asked.

"Something you may have heard from your uncle?"

Archie thought for a moment.

"There is one thing."

He said.

"A while ago, we met up in London for a drink. We were chatting, and he mentioned something to do with a friend of

Rebecca's and an exam. I cannot really remember now, but he was saying how strong Rebecca had been as she had reported her friend."

"For what? For cheating?"

"Well. I do not know. It was a while ago. But Rebecca somehow overcame her friendship to do the right thing. That was what he said."

"Hmmm," Sebastien murmured. "Most interesting."

"Of course, it could have been to do with one of the other two."

Sebastien turned to him. "What other two?"

He asked.

"Oh. Did I not say? Luke also said that Rebecca had betrayed Kate and Daniel as well. I do not know who they are. I am guessing they are her friends as well. Well, they were."

"Most intriguing, is it not?"

Sebastien commented.

"Are all these people still invited to the party? After your cousin has apparently betrayed them? And why did they come? Most intriguing indeed."

"We don't know that Kate and Daniel are at the party."

Archie corrected him.

"Yes, suppose you are right. I just assumed. But if they are, then my questions still stand."

"Well, enjoy it."

Said Archie.

"It is going to be the most interesting thing to happen this weekend."

"Perhaps."

Sebastien said.

"Perhaps."

Quiet for a moment. Archie cut in.

"How was Samantha? By the way? You two seemed to be getting along together earlier."

"Yes. She was very nice. We talked about her work. Turns out she is a nurse."

"Oh yes."

Said Archie. Remembering.

"In London?"

"At St. Thomas Hospital."

"Of course. It has been so long now I forgot. We have only met once before. Years ago. As I said, I do not see any of them often."

"Clearly"

Sebastien agreed.

"And how was her husband? You seemed to be getting on well with him?"

"Richard? Yes, he was fine. We just chatted, really. We talked a bit about football and rugby, then about craft beer. After, I asked him if he had been to Exeter or Plymouth before, as we were nearby. He said he had not been to Exeter in years but had been to Plymouth not long ago. He enjoyed the Barbican Waterfront. Not long after, I left to go to my room. So yes, pleasant enough."

"Good"

"He is a farmer, I think."

Archie commented.

"That's what Uncle Tony said."

"Well, perhaps this trip will not be as bad as you thought."

Sebastien suggested.

Archie looked at him skeptically.

"Do not doubt me yet. They have not started drinking."

Sebastien laughed.

"Oh, Archie. How cynical you are."

"Aha."

Archie declared.

"I almost forgot to say. The reason I came over in the first place is to tell you there is a drinks party downstairs. It's starting soon, I think."

He looked at his phone for the time.

"Ok"

Sebastien replied.

"I will get finished up and then come down."

"Do you want me to wait for you?"

Archie asked.

"No. I will be fine. This house is not that big. I am sure I will be able to find the way… eventually."

Archie smiled and got up to leave the room.

CHAPTER 14

"She knows. I do not know how, but she does!"

Kate is frantic. Is terrified. How could she know? How is it possible? Could she have seen them? Around his work, maybe? Or had she heard it from someone? But if so, who? Kate had not told anyone about this. She had told no one. She did not think he would. It would ruin everything for him. His family. His happy life. No. He would not have told anyone. It is just so confusing. How could she possibly know?

All these thoughts are whirling through Kate's head. She has caught Tony, pulling him into a side room. She needs to speak to him. She does not know what to do.

"Are you sure?"
He asks
"Yes. She told me. She was talking to me about forbidden

love. An affair. It feels so right. But needing to tell the truth. Because it is wrong. Because you must do the right thing. God. She knows. She knows. What are we going to do?"

"Steady now."

Says Tony in a calming voice, putting his hands on her arms and staring straight into her eyes. "Everything will be okay. It will all be fine. If she knows, she did not confront you about it. Did she? That implies that she does not intend to make it public. So, there we are. It is all going to be fine."

Kate looked at him. How could he be so calm? So rational? If this all came out, it would be far worse for him. God, what had happened to them? This was only meant to be a bit of fun.

It all started on a rainy afternoon, quite by chance. Kate was working at the café. He comes in for a coffee. They recognize each other. They start with simple small talk. He asks how she is finding London. She asked him about his work. Before you know it, they find themselves in bed. Christ. This was never meant to happen and never meant to come back to haunt them like this. It was never meant to come to Dartmoor. To Claytons. God. Kate does not know if she can take it. If she will be able to keep it up.

"But we do not know that, do we?

Kate says.

"Maybe she just did not want to face it? What if later she decides she cannot lie anymore? Cannot keep it to herself? What then? Then they all get hurt. My parents. Your wife. I was already dreading this weekend. Having to see Imogen and having to pretend. Deceiving and betraying her. I am sleeping with her husband, and here she is, kindly offering me drinks. It just makes me feel so guilty. I feel so terrible. I could not bear for her to find out. God. What the hell are we going to do?"

"Just calm down."

Tony said sternly.

"Listen. Do not worry about Imogen. She is still my wife. I still belong to her. We have just had fun. You were, no offence, just a distraction—an exciting, thrilling experience. I suspect I was very much the same for you. So, you have nothing to be guilty about. I still love Imogen. That is not going to change."

He paused.

"If you really think she knows. If you really think she might tell, you must talk to her."

Kate stared at him.

"Me? Why should I talk to her? Why don't you do it? You are related to her."

"Exactly. That is why I can't. Being related makes it more likely that she will react negatively. You, on the other hand, are her friend—someone she trusts. You are more likely to get through to her that this is nothing. It's just a fling. That Imogen does not need to know. That neither does anyone else, for that matter."

Kate was unsure. What if it backfired? What if she got angry? She decided she could not take it anymore. Decided to tell everyone? What would we do then?

"Hey."

He said softly, sensing her nerves and putting an arm on her shoulder.

"It will all be okay. Just talk to her. Reason with her. Convince her. It will all sort itself out. We just need to be strong."

Was he right? Could he be right? Maybe. Maybe talking to her would do the trick. Or maybe it would not. Maybe it would ruin everything. Oh God. This is a nightmare.

CHAPTER 15

aving changed into his dinner jacket, Sebastien felt a bit more relaxed.

It is not the usual reaction to changing into formal dinner wear, at least not for him. But here, it is calming. Now he feels properly dressed. Well prepared for the ordeal ahead. As if he is in a uniform. Blending into the crowd.

He must admit, Kiera had got it right. It did fit perfectly. How had she done it, though? That is what Sebastien did not understand. Had he just not noticed her sizing him up every time they met? Had she made a quick mental note every time his back was turned? And then there was the inside leg. Surely, he would have noticed if she was looking at that area. Yes, it was puzzling.

Leaving his room, Sebastien heard light footsteps coming towards him. The gentle clicks that you hear from someone wearing heels. Turning to his right, he saw a beautiful young woman. She was blonde with long hair. Slim and average height. She was wearing a close-fitting, silk evening gown in a dark red.

Seeing him, she smiled. Displaying beautiful white teeth.

"Hello"
She said in a cheerful, almost mocking tone.
"So, who are you then?"

She made an exaggerated suspicious look, clearly for comic effect.

"I have not seen you before. Are you a thief? A spy?"
Seeing me slightly startled, she burst into a laugh. High pitched like a teenager.
"I am sorry. I could not resist. I am Jessica, by the way. So, who are you?"
"Sebastien."
I replied.
"I am a friend of Archie's. I have come with him for the weekend."
"Oh, right. Yes, I heard Archie had brought a friend along. Nobody told me that you were going to be so handsome, though."
I blushed. Causing Jessica's smile to increase. She clearly had a mischievous nature. She enjoys pushing the boundaries

of what she can get away with. And I suspect she enjoyed the recognition of her beauty. Who doesn't?

"So,"

Jessica said, starting to walk.

"Are you enjoying your time here? Or do you wish you could leave already? Get away from the madhouse?"

She asked teasingly.

"It has been very nice, thank you. Your aunt has a lovely house. In such a beautiful place as well."

"Yes,"

Jessica pondered.

"It is beautiful here. The moor. The rocks. There is nowhere quite like it."

She lingered on the thought.

"Have you always lived here?"

I asked.

"At Claytons? No. I have always lived at Dartmoor. I only moved to Claytons when I was nine. My parents died."

"I am sorry."

I said sympathetically.

"Thank you. It was a long time ago now. I have moved on. But I still wish they could be here." She paused for a moment. Caught up in her longing. Her sadness was clearly taking over her mind. "Anyway," She said. Changing the subject. "I do not live here now. I moved to London about a year ago, and I am studying at Royal Holloway."

"Oh, excellent. What is it that you study?"

"Fashion design."

She replied. Brightly.

"That is brilliant. And are you enjoying your course?"

"Oh yes. It is so inspiring. So creative. I love thinking of things to wear. I always have done, since I was little. I was always trying on my mum's clothes. And the Aunt Im's."

"Well. It sounds like you have certainly chosen the right path."

"Yes. I cannot imagine studying anything else. It is my dream, really. And what about you? What do you do?"

"I am a psychotherapist."

"A therapist. That must be interesting. Having people reveal to you all their deepest, darkest desires."

"Well, there are many things we do. We use talking therapy and other methods to help our patients. But yes. Sometimes, it is our deepest, darkest desires that cause us the most harm. Sometimes, we need to explore them. That is, we need to explore those things we cannot admit sometimes. Whether they are our desires or our sins, guilt can be the most damaging of them all."

"Yes"

She replied. Pausing for a moment.

"Can I ask you something?"

Sebastien hesitated. Unsure where this was going and slightly concerned by that.

"Of course,"

He said gently.

"If someone was selfish. I mean, really selfish. They had acted in ways that had really hurt others. Others that we thought they cared about. Could they be helped by therapy?"

Sebastien considered this for a moment.

"In what way do you mean?"

He asked softly.

"Do you mean help them to make amends for the things they have done wrong? Or, to help them cope with the guilt?"

"No"
Replied Jessica.
"I mean to help them feel empathy for their actions. To feel remorse, I suppose."
Sebastien considered this carefully.
"I guess this is possible. We could examine why they did these actions. What was their justification? Then, look at how they affected others. Ask them to consider the impact of their actions. Then, we can see how this makes them feel. Of course, there is no guarantee that they will feel empathy or remorse. Some people simply lack empathy."
Jessica nodded and considered this. Her brow creased in thought.
"In terms of coping with guilt? Can it help you do that as well?"
She asked.
"Yes. We can explore their feelings. Understand why they are feeling that way. And from that, we can go on the path to making them feel better."
Jessica nodded again.
"Is there any way I can help you?"
I asked.
"Is there someone you would wish me to speak to? To try and help?"
Jessica shook her head.
"No. Thank you. It was just hypothetical, really. I was just curious. But thank you for asking."
She said. An unconfident smile on her face. As if her mind was elsewhere. All this supported Sebastien's belief that there was more to this question than she said. Considering what he had heard. He had a good idea as to whom it related.

"We all have to take responsibility sometimes, don't we?"
She added.

"We all have to do what is right. What is best for others? And perhaps what is also best for ourselves? Don't you agree?"

Sebastien turned slightly to her. Slowing his pace.

"Yes. We all must do what is right. It may be uncomfortable, but it must be done."

She nodded, smiling.

"Do you like theatre?"

She asked him cheerfully. Putting her arms through mine. A wide smile grew on her face.

I was startled for a moment. This is quite a drastic change in subject. It had taken me quite by surprise. But perhaps it shouldn't have. When we feel uncomfortable. When a subject gets too close, we like to change the subject. To change the focus onto a new topic. One that is not so deep.

"Yes"

I replied as we made our way down the stairs.

"It is nice to go to the theatre every once in a while. Do you?"

"Oh yes"

She beamed.

"I love it. That is one of the great things about living in London and having the West End on your doorstep. It is just magical. I recently saw a play at the Northcott Theatre in Exeter. I was there visiting a friend. That was brilliant as well. You know, I do some acting?"

"Really?"

I was intrigued.

"How excellent. What plays have you appeared in?"

"Oh, it is only am dram, but I do love it. It is so freeing, so liberating, being someone else. And it is so much fun. We do have such a laugh."

She said, grinning and guiding me through the corridor. I am guessing towards the drinks party.

"I have been in King Lear. The Importance of Being Ernest. Much Ado About Nothing. Oh, it is so much fun. And apparently, I am not bad at it. Our teacher says I should try for some real parts?"

"Really? That is impressive. Do you think you will?"

"Oh, I do not know. I still want to go into fashion. But I do like acting, though. Who knows what the future holds?"

Her voice took a mystical tone.

"Whatever it is, I wish you all the best with it."

"Thank you."

Getting closer now, they could hear the sound of voices. Yes. The party had begun.

CHAPTER 16

Once they had arrived, Jessica split off to talk to another young woman across the room. She and all the other women were dressed in fine silk evening gowns. Like the kind you would wear to prom, but perhaps just a bit classier. The men were all dressed in dinner jackets, with black bow ties and white cotton shirts. It was clear that this family liked to celebrate their occasions in a formal manner. They liked to do things the old-fashioned way. Something about this intrigued Sebastien as if he were observing some far-away aboriginal tribe. He saw a different way of doing things from what he was used to. A way from a different age.

Seeing Sebastien had entered the room, Archie came over to join him.

"So, you found your way, alright then? Didn't go stumbling into a closet or something?"

"Yes. I met Jessica in the corridor."

Replied Sebastien. Gesturing to her.

"And she showed me the way."

"Oh yes. She is a great girl, isn't she?"

"Yes."

Sebastien agreed.

"She was very pleasant."

Thinking that maybe Archie regarded her more highly than he said.

"Right."

Said Archie seriously.

"Come on, let's get it over with. We can say hello, and then we can do our own thing."

"Come on, cheer up. You might enjoy talking to them."

Sebastien suggested.

Archie gave him a doubtful look.

"Nice try. They are either old, people I do not know or people who are not interested in me."

Now, Sebastien gave him a doubtful look.

"That is not really fair, is it? I mean, the evening has only just started."

"And the sooner it ends, the better."

Sebastien continued his look.

"Do not look at me like that. It is just uncomfortable. You see why I wanted you here now?"

"Oh, I thought it was because I had always dreamed of seeing Dartmoor?"

"Well, I could hardly say the truth, could I? Anyway, you did say you would like to see Dartmoor."

"Only after you asked me. It was hardly a lifelong dream."

"That is beside the point. You said you would like to see Dartmoor. I have brought you. There it is. It is all great. Now, come on. Let's get it over with."

Archie pulled Sebastien in the direction of the other guests.

Moving across the room. Sebastien was able to take in the atmosphere fully. The room was dark, with bright lamps in each corner. Reminding him of a jazz club. From what he could see, the room had dark blue wallpaper—a few book-cases filled with leather-bound volumes. Around the edges, high-backed leather chairs and polished side tables are used. In the middle was a large space where we all mingled. Moving between us, some staff dressed in shirts and ties. Carrying champagne coupes and canapes on silver trays. It felt like it should be in the 1930's. Something about the nostalgia of the event did please Sebastien. It was an interesting aspect of the party he had been press-ganged into attending.

Having moved across the room, they now reached a huddle of other men. Sebastien recognized Tony and Richard from before. Two other men were standing with them. Younger. He would guess about late teens or early twenties. One was muscular with thick brown hair and a strong jaw. The other was still physically fit but more athletic, with blond hair and an attractive, well-proportioned face.

"Sebastien, you met Richard and Uncle Tony before."
They both nodded towards me.
"This is Luke."
He said, gesturing to the athletic one.
"And Daniel."
Gesturing to the other.
"They are two friends of Rebecca's from school."
Turning them, he said.
"This is Sebastien. A friend of mine who has joined me for the trip."
"Pleased to meet you."
Luke said, offering his hand. A tight smile appeared on his face. I sensed it was from anxiety rather than hostility. Whether it was that he was anxious about me, I could not tell.

Thinking back. I think Archie said it was someone called Luke with whom Rebecca had been arguing earlier. That may explain his anxiety. After having a row like that, to then have to make polite conversation. Celebrating their birthday like nothing had happened. Yes, he could quite well understand his nerves.

"Thank you."
Sebastien replied.
"You as well."

Daniel just nodded in my direction, looking me up and down. Yes, it was clear to see the type of person he was. The arrogance came off him like a stench. Clearly, he believed I was not important enough to even shake hands with. With Daniels's attention gone, I gave a quick look to Archie. He raised his eyebrows in a slight shrug. His way of saying, 'Yes, I know. He is a dick'.

"So, as I was saying. It is about being varied. Cardio. Power. Speed. Flexibility. To succeed at Rugby, you need to master these. The key is to develop a workout routine where you develop all these, not just one."

Ah, sport. The one thing you can rely on men for is that they will be able to bond over it. It was not hard to tell that Rugby and his associated training for it would be Daniel's specialist subject. I have nothing against rugby. It is a great sport and enjoyable to watch. I do not want to play it. It's the same as me not wanting to get into a boxing ring. It just gets boring when someone makes the sport their whole personality. Worse still, they use it to show themselves as being superior to others; this was what I feared I was seeing before me. At least he was not interested in me. Making him easy to avoid. I sense that Richard and Tony were not so lucky.

"Yes."
Said Tony, smiling. His default position. Making it hard to tell if he was actually interested in the conversation or not.
"I remember playing rugby in my university days. It was jolly good fun."
"Well, yes. It should be fun. But it is more than that. It is a way of life if you do it properly. If you want to win."
Daniel replied.

Oh, Christ. Sebastien thought. If he is going to talk like this all evening, I may have to pretend to get a headache and retire early. That might not be a bad idea in general, actually. Archie would kill me, leaving him here alone. Better still.

"It is hard."
Daniel continued. Unfortunately.
"Outside London, it can be hard to find a proper gym— one with all the right facilities. To ensure you continue your routine. That being said. I went to that great, big, modern one in Exeter recently. I must say, that was good."
"St Sidwell's? Yes, it is excellent. State of the art."
Tony said.
"And very eco-friendly."
Luke added.
"Yes, I swam there. It was great. Very clean, and a good length too."
Richard said.

Just then, Jessica and another young woman joined the group. The other girl was slim and had chestnut brown hair.

"What is this? You boring everyone with constant gym talk."
Said Jessica mischievously. Looking towards Daniel.
"Boring? I am not boring anyone. It is just a man's thing. Something you would not understand."

And there is another flaw to add to the list. Thought Sebastien. At this rate, we would need two pages.

"I would not understand, sport? Really? I was in our sixth-form netball team."

"I mean a real sport."

"Oh, it is not a real sport, is it? Just because we do not want to get dementia in thirty years from so many hits to the head."

"Now, now."

Said Tony. Playing peacemaker.

"I do not think these two have met?"

He said. Gesturing to me and the other girl.

"Why don't you introduce them?"

He said to Jessica, clearly wanting to change the subject.

It worked.

"Sebastien"

She said.

"This is Kate. My best friend since we were tiny."

Wrapping her arms tightly around the woman. Kate smiled both affectionately but with a slight discomfort.

"Pleased to meet you"

Kate said. Offering me a hand. Once she had managed to prise it free from Jessica's grip.

"Yes. Pleased to meet you as well."

I said, shaking. I was unsure whether I should do the customary kiss on the cheek as she had just offered her hand. These things could be hard to tell.

"So, are you enjoying the party?"

She asked.

"Yes"

Sebastien replied.

"It is very nice to be here."

The attention of the whole group was now focused on him. This was not what he wanted at all. He wanted just to blend into the background. Be unnoticeable. Not the centre of attention.

After a slight pause. Archie said

"Ah, I do not think you have met the birthday girl yet."

Seeing Rebecca moving towards them. Leaving Imogen and Samantha to talk amongst themselves.

"Rebecca"

He said. Beckoning her forward.

"This is Sebastien. My friend, who I brought with me this weekend."

"Good to meet you."

She says. Her voice even. A small smile appeared on her face. She offered me her hand.

"Yes, good to meet you as well. Happy birthday"

I said. Shaking her hand. Certain that, in this case, a kiss would not be welcomed.

Meeting her. I can see what Archie meant. She is polite, but there is a bit of disinterest there. It's not as obvious as Daniels, but, like Archie said, it's just a feeling. As if, her focus is fixed on another, more important target.

"Are you enjoying Dartmoor?"

She asks without much enthusiasm.

"Yes. It is a beautiful place. I have always wanted to come."

I said. Sticking to the story, Archie gave me.

"You must have enjoyed growing up here."

I added.

After a pause, Rebecca said.

"Yes. It was pleasant. There is nowhere really quite like here."

Looking around her. As if she could see through the walls and out onto the moor itself.

As the conversation went forward, the topic changed—the focus following it onto the others. I was relieved. It already felt awkward being in this house with all these strangers. The least I hoped for was just to slip into the background. To blend in. I glanced at Archie, smiling back at him. It is good I like you so much, I thought. Otherwise, I would be in the first taxi out of here.

CHAPTER 17

Fifteen minutes had passed, and the party was in full swing. The room had developed a certain energy. A buzz made of chatter and laughter.

The guests had formed into three groups. In the middle, all the younger ones formed a huddle. Jessica, Rebecca, Daniel, Kate and Luke were all stood together. From the constant voices and occasional laughter, it would appear to be going well. Perhaps the drink had made them forget their previous troubles. Or at least dulled them for the moment.

To the right-hand side was Imogen, Tony and Richard. Their conversation was not as animated as the central group but was engaging them all.

Then, to the left were Sebastien, Archie and Samantha. It

had been a pleasant discussion, Sebastien thought. Just small talk really about parts of their lives they shared in common. Restaurants and bars they knew in London. There is a bit of discussion about their childhoods. They told me about their aunt and uncle. A bit of politics came in somewhere. It did not stay too long, thankfully. It's just easy to talk, really. All surface level. Nothing too deep.

"You know, I just really feel like eating some sausages."

Samatha said quite unexpectedly. While sipping her orange juice.

"I am not normally bothered about them, but I just really fancy them. I could not get enough of those little cocktail canapes."

"Yes, they were scrummy."

Archie remarked.

"I always used to love having bangers and mash when I was a child. What about you, Seb? Did you used to love bangers and mash?"

Sebastien gave his friend a skeptical look.

"You know I cannot stand sausages."

He said.

"I know you can't now, but I did not know if that was just an adult thing. Like when I was a kid, I loved sherbet lemons. But now. They are way too sweet. I thought maybe you only developed your insanity once you had reached eighteen."

Samantha made a small giggle.

Looking briefly over into the room. Sebastien saw a server move past the other two groups. Carrying a silver tray of champagne coupes. Having offered drinks to the younger group in the middle, he turned to return to the kitchen. But having changed her mind, Jessica took a glass when the server's head was turned. Nearly causing the poor man to spill the tray. They erupted into laughter, momentarily catching the attention of the rest of us.

"I think you will find I am completely sane."
Sebastien replied. Returning to his friend.
"It is you two who are not. I cannot understand how you like it."
"Oh, come on. It is gorgeous."
Archie said.
"I will have to find some more of those canapes to rid you of your phobia."
"Bring those near me, and the cocktail stick will end up in your eye."
Sebastien warned.

Just then, we heard a gagging sound. It was quiet at first. Appearing soft. It's like someone just had a sore throat. But soon, it became more intense. The sound became louder, as if someone was choking. As if they were struggling to breathe.

We turned forward to see Jessica. Looking breathless and clearly starting to choke. With her hand to her chest.

"Jess, are you alright?"

Asked Kate. Her concern was clear from her voice.

Continuing to choke, Jess looked at her. She dropped her glass. Took a slight stumble back before collapsing to the floor. Her arm broke her fall before she fell back, flat against the ground.

Suddenly, we all rushed over. Uncertain at what had just happened and scared as to what it meant.

"Jessica, what is the matter?"
Tony asked.
"Just breathe, darling. Just breathe"
Imogen said calmly.
"Oh my god. What is happening?"
Kate screamed.

After a few seconds, she clutched her neck. Her choking became louder and more rapid. Her throat sounded dryer. It becoming increasingly clear that now she could not breathe. She then started trembling. Her whole body is vibrating. Her head nodding and twisting violently. Frothing appeared in her mouth. Her arms and legs trembling ferociously. She was having a seizure. She had lost complete control over her body.

"She is fitting. She is having a seizure. Give her some air."
Samantha commanded.

We all moved slightly back. But not much. Frozen by what was happening. Out of concern. Horror. Morbid curiosity.

Grabbing her mouth. Samantha held it in place. Preventing the girl from biting her tongue.

"She needs an ambulance. Call one now."

Tony moved to leave the room. But as he stood up, it was clear it was too late. She suddenly stopped moving. Stopped choking. Her skin turned pale. Her eyes glazed over.

Samantha put two fingers to her neck. Feeling her pulse. After a second, her face collapsed. A look of despair on her face.

"She is dead."

The whole room released a gasp. They were all in shock. Then the room erupted.

"No"
Imogen whaled. Falling into Tony's arms. He embraced her tightly. Her head was buried into his chest. His eyes fixed on the corpse.
"Oh"
Murmured Kate. Standing up from her crouched position. Stumbling over to the wall. Resting on it with one arm for support.

Samantha closed Jessica's eyes—a single tear rolling down her cheek.

Richard was holding her leg. He seemed fixed in shock. His eyes were wide and glued to the body.

Luke started sobbing. His head in his hands.

Daniel and Rebecca just stood there. Motionless. Their faces were blank as if they were struggling to process what had just happened and how they should react.

Archie was also frozen. His mouth is open. His eyes fixed on her. He was in complete shock.

Next to him, Sebastien was tense. How had this happened? He thought. How can she have just died? A healthy young woman? And why did she choke? Why did she fit? Was it some form of epilepsy? Was she poisoned? What had happened? He then returned to one of his first questions—a healthy young woman. A sudden sadness came over him. He remembered talking to her on the stairs. Her dreams of fashion. Of becoming a great designer. Her cheeky, funny attitude. God, what a waste.

They all stood there silent for a moment. Collectively still.

"We need to leave."
Said Tony uncomfortably.
"We need to call the police and leave her here. There is nothing else we can do. Come on"
He said. Moving Imogen towards the door.

After looking at him, the rest silently followed. Their shock, putting them into a temporary state of complete obedience.

Moving towards the door, Sebastien's mind was full of so many questions. So many answers that needed to be found.

CHAPTER 18

Once they had all left, the doors were closed behind them. They moved through the corridor and into the lounge. They were still in a state of shock. It just was impossible. How could she be dead? Jessica. Just a few minutes ago, she had been laughing and joking. Being her joyful, happy, cheeky self. Now, she was on the floor. Barely cold.

"So, what happened?"

Demanded Samantha. Facing Kate, Daniel and Luke. Her face was red. Her voice was strong. Her passion and anger flowed through it. Her eyes were as sharp as daggers.

"What do you mean, what happened?"

Replied Daniel.

"We don't know."

"You don't know?"

Samantha repeated. Looking at each of them in turn.

"Seriously. My cousin drops dead, and you don't know. You were the ones near her. How could you not know?"

"She just started choking."

Said Kate. Her voice breaking.

"Nothing happened. She just started choking. Then she fell. Then she started…shaking."

She appeared to be lost in the memory. The grief was clear on her face.

"She did not just start choking."

Shouted Samantha.

"She was clearly poisoned."

Everyone shot her a glance.

"Poisoned?"

Said Daniel skeptically.

"Are you sure you are not imagining things?"

He said in a patronizing tone.

"Am I imagining things? How bloody dare you!"

Samantha hit back.

"A healthy young woman starts choking, falls to the ground and dies. You do not have to be a genius to figure out something suspicious has happened."

She looked at him as if she might strangle him.

"How exactly would you explain it?"

"I don't know."

Daniel blustered.

"But come on. Really. Poisoned. Who would want to poison her?"

"I don't know."

Samantha agreed.

"I cannot think of any reason why someone would want to hurt her. Let alone kill her. But obviously, someone did."

"Could it have been an epileptic fit?"
Kate asked.
"Couldn't that explain it?"
"No"
Said Samantha.
"Epilepsy does not cause choking. She could have likely had a seizure if it was an epileptic fit. But not the choking first. Having a seizure could cause choking. But we all saw she choked first, then started fitting. It was not epilepsy."

They all looked around at each other. Unsure what to think. Samantha stood confidently in a striking pose. She was on a mission. Both Kate and Daniel were standing in front of her. Together, they formed a triangle. They were uncomfortable but focused on the enraged woman. Luke was slumped in a chair behind them. Next to the fire. His eyes are still red from crying. Imogen was sat on the chair opposite. She had composed herself but looked heartbroken. She barely seemed to be noticing anything that was going on. Tony stood behind her. His hand was on her shoulder. To his left stood Rebecca. Still emotionless. Both Sebastien and Archie were behind Samantha. Still by the door. Watching the events unfold.

"So, who was it?"
Said Samantha harshly.
"Which one of you did it?"
She said, looking at the three suspects in front of her.
"Which one of us did it?"
Replied Kate. Her face turned red.
"You think one of us did this."
"Of course, one of you did!"

Samantha screamed.

"Who else would?"

"But we would never hurt her."

Kate screamed back.

"At least I never would."

"What is that supposed to mean!"

Shouted Daniel furiously.

"Nothing. I just meant I would never hurt her. She was my best friend. I just cannot believe she is gone."

Kate's voice broke towards the end. She started to cry.

"How could you believe that we would want to kill her?"

Shouted Luke. Rising from his chair and moving forward.

"Jess was the most kind-hearted, beautiful, funny person I have ever met. She was just perfect. Why would we want to hurt her? How could you think that we could ever hurt her? We would never do it."

"Well, someone did!"

Samantha screamed. Facing them all and turning to them one by one.

"She was stood by you all when she collapsed. One of you must have done it."

Behind them, they heard a smash. The rest momentarily turned before refocusing on the drama in front of them. Sebastien decided to see what had happened. Archie followed him. As they moved out into the hall, they could hear sweeping to the right. Archie moved in this direction, leading them to the kitchen. Here, they could see Richard sweeping some broken glass off the floor. He moved swiftly to the bin. Tipping in the contents.

"Sorry"

He said, embarrassed.

"I just came in to get some water, and it slipped out of my hands. I do not know what came over me?"

"I would not worry."

Sebastien reassured him.

"It has been a difficult night for us all."

"It is just awful. Just unbelievable. One moment, she was there talking, and the next, she was dead."

Richard said. Staring at the space in front of him. Completely absorbed by his thoughts.

"How could this happen? Why did a brilliant young woman just die?"

His emotion entered his voice.

Sebastien and Archie looked at each other. They both knew that they did not know the answer.

"That is something that none of us know yet."

Sebastien said calmly.

"But we will. Hopefully soon"

Richard looks at them both. Searching their eyes. As if they could give him an answer.

"Perhaps you should see your wife."

Sebastien suggested gently.

"She seems very upset. Very angry. She needs a rock. A shoulder to cry on. She needs you."

Richard takes a deep breath and straightens himself.

"Yes. How selfish of me. Of course, she must be distraught. I hope she will be ok."

"No. You are not selfish. You went through a traumatic experience as well, as we all did. But now."

Sebastien said, gesturing to the door.

"It is the time for you to be there for her."

Smiling at them, Richard went to the door. Going in the direction of the lounge as he left.

"God. It is terrible, though, isn't it?"

Archie said.

"Such a nice young girl."

He turned to his friend.

"Do you think Samantha was right? That she was poisoned?"

Sebastien hesitated for a moment.

"It is right that healthy young women do not just collapse randomly."

He said.

"Whether or not she was poisoned is something that we cannot be certain of yet, but it is certainly a possibility. If not the most likely possibility."

"Good god."

Archie said, his face showing his shock.

"But who would want to kill her? She was such a nice girl."

"Good people are murdered sometimes."

Sebastien remarked.

"Not just the bad ones."

He paused for a moment in thought.

"To understand why it happened, we must first fully understand how it happened."

He looked Archie straight in the eyes. "We must go back to the scene of the crime."

"What?"

Archie exclaimed.

"We can't go in there. It is a crime scene. There is a dead body in there. Isn't there a law against that or something?"

Sebastien shrugged, cocking his head to one side.

"The police have not arrived yet. They have not formally sealed the scene. How are we meant to know not to go in there?"

"Sebastien!"

Archie said sternly.

"Do you want to know what happened?"

Sebastien asked Archie. His voice was serious.

"Yes"

Archie replied nervously.

"Well, as I said, to do that, we must first understand how it happened. That means we must go back."

Archie hesitated. He knew it was wrong. You were not supposed just to go wandering into murder scenes. But Sebastien was right. He did want to know what happened, why she died. And they would only find that out if they went back to where it happened.

"Okay"

He said reluctantly.

"But if we are caught, I am saying you forced me to do it."

"Oh, I would expect nothing less."

CHAPTER 19

They all walk out of the lounge. They are exhausted, both by the death itself and the argument that erupted in the aftermath. They all have the same thoughts. How could this be happening? How can it be real? How can she really be gone?

They are all leaving like mindless drones and not thinking about where they are going or what they are doing. Too consumed by their other thoughts. Whether it is to their rooms to escape this living nightmare through their dreams. Or to a quiet corner of the house to dwell on their sorrows festering within them. They move automatically. Without thought. Absorbed by their trauma. By the shared trauma they had all experienced.

As Kate makes her way to her room, she feels something grab her arm. Before she can protest, she is pulled through a door into a side room. The door is shut. She turns around. She can see it is Tony who has brought her in here. Oh God, she thinks. Not now. I do not want to do this now.

"Tony, what are you doing?" asks Kate. Her voice is weak. She feels exhausted. Shattered. She just wants to sleep. To get away from all of this.

Turning to her, he fixes his gaze on her, looking straight into her eyes. Filled with suspicion.

"Did you do something?"
He asks.

Kate stares back at him, stunned for a moment. She cannot believe what she is hearing.

"Excuse me?"
"Did you do something? Did you do something to Jessica?"
"NO"
She shouted, her rage filling her.
"Of course, I did not. How could you think that? Jessica and I were best friends."
He eyed her skeptically.
"If you did do something."

He says calmly and slowly as if he is dealing with a child—one who may boil over at any minute into a rage.

"Then it is best to say now. I can help. We can sort it out. Just tell me."

You patronizing bastard, she thinks.

"I just told you. I did not do anything. Why would I? Protecting our secret is not worth more to me than her."

"All I know is I told you to talk to her about this, and now she is dead." He pauses, his face flushed. "I said to talk to her, not kill her!"

"Did you know? Oh, how gracious of you."

She spat out.

"Why did you do it? Don't you see what you have done? It will all come out now. What happened between us? Our affair. The police will find out. Christ, why did you kill her? Surely, you must have known it would make everything worse."

She could not believe this.

"For god's sake. Jessica is lying there, dead on the floor, and all you care about is us, whether your precious wife finds out. Your wretched daughter. How can you think about that? She is dead."

Her voice breaks. She heaves, and her eyes well up. She turns away and wipes them.

"It is easier for you. No marriage. No family. No reputation. You have nothing to lose. I am not so fortunate."

Yes, you did have more to lose, didn't you? She thinks.

"Listen. I did not kill her. Okay? For the record, I was going to talk to her. Try to make her understand, as you said. What I did not do was poison her at your daughter's birthday party. Okay?

He looks at her. He then looks down and nods quickly.

"Okay. I'm sorry. I believe you."

She breathes, relaxing. At least he got there eventually.

"Listen"

He says, becoming more animated. His mind is working fast.

"We need to keep our secret. We need to not tell anyone about us."

She looks at him, astonished.

"What? You just said they would find out about everything. All the stuff we have done. How will us denying it help?"

"Listen. I know that is what I said before. But I was panicking. I thought you might have killed her. That you could be a murderer. But I believe you now. I know you did not do it. So that means that we can contain this."

He looked at her, wanting a sign of acknowledgement. She was still astounded. She could not believe what she was hearing.

"Jessica was the only person who knew."

He continued.

"No one else did. So that gives us an opportunity. If we tell them about us. About everything we did. Admit everything. Then that is it. My family will know, and so will yours. All our fears before. They will all come true. If we remain silent, however. Then we have a chance. I know people in London. People who will remove the evidence of our meetings. CCTV, Hotel bookings, dinner reservations. If we remain silent. If we give them time. Then we can contain this. We can prevent this from becoming public."

Kate was silent. She was just speechless. How could he be so cold? So calculating? His niece, a girl he has had guardianship of since she was nine years old, is dead. Instead of mourning her. Grieving. He is here. Plotting how to save his skin. It is disgusting. I mean, was I really so blind? Was all that charm, that sensitivity he showed me an act? Was he really just this all along? I do not know. Right now, Kate does not know what to think. I mean, could he have done it? Did he kill her? Was that what this was all about? All of this.

Bringing her in here, accusing her, and declaring that she has ruined everything. That they are now doomed to be exposed. Then, only to say that he believes her. That they can solve this. If they stay silent, he can get rid of the evidence of their affair so that no one will ever find out. Was that all a tactic? A way to manipulate her into following his plan. To conceal his motive? Again, I am not sure. But how could he do it? He was nowhere near Jessica when she died. How… Oh God. Of course. I mean, it could be the case. It is certainly possible.

"So?"
Tony says, interrupting her thoughts.
"Will you stay quiet? Give me time to sort this out?"

Sensing her doubt, he touches her arm. She tenses.
"Listen,"
He says gently.
"Just trust me. Give me some time, and I can sort this out for both of us. I can make sure neither of our fears come true."

Trust you. She thinks. Never again. But she does wonder. If he is involved. If he is responsible for Jessica's murder, then where does that leave me? Now Jessica is gone, and I am the only person who knows about us. I am the last loose end. So, if I refuse to stay quiet, say that I will tell them everything. What would he do? Would he kill me? I would not put it past him. The one thing he has shown here is that he will take any opportunity he can to save himself. To cover his mistakes. Okay. I know what I need to do. It is the only way I can be sure I will be safe.

She looks at him, her eyes wide, like a child, and nods meekly.

"Okay"

She says quietly.

"Yes. I will do it. I will tell them nothing."

Tony smiles.

"Good girl. Do not worry. I will sort everything out. Just leave it to me."

He embraces her in a hug.

She feels as if he is suffocating her in his grip. Yes, she thinks. You will sort everything out, won't you? The real question is, to what lengths are you willing to go?

CHAPTER 20

Entering the room again, Archie begins to feel sick. She is still there. Her body sprawled on the floor. Her face is contorted, although it is now slightly relaxed. Now, the muscles are no longer working. Looking at it, Archie begins to doubt his judgement. Should he really have let Sebastien persuade him to do this? I mean, we are not detectives. We do not work for the police. I make craft beer, and he talks to people for a living. Well, he listens to them, really. They should not be here. It is not their job. Saying that it does feel right. Being here. They both want to know what happened, how it was that this beautiful young woman ended up dead. Despite the fact that he knows he shouldn't, that it is not really their place, and that he feels a bit queasy. Archie does want to be there. He wants to know who killed her.

Having just entered the room, Sebastien stops, just staring at the body for a few moments. He then goes over to the side of the body and crouches down. His eyes move down the body from head to toe, taking it all in. He then gets up and wanders just slightly backward to where the glass had been dropped.

Taking his eyes away, allowing himself a moment to breathe and compose himself, Archie goes over to one of the side tables. Looking down, he sees a tumbler of yellow-coloured liquid. Picking it up, he smelled tequila. It must have been left by one of the others when they all left the room.

"Tequila."
He says, turning back around to Sebastien and raising the glass so he can see.
"The devil's tipple. That is what my grandmother used to call it."

Sebastien does not raise his head. His eyes are fixed on the glass on the floor, as is his attention.

"I think, my friend, that this is Lucifer's tipple tonight."
Lowering his head, he puts his nose to the glass, smelling its contents.
"Almonds"
He murmurs.
"Cyanide?"
Archie asks.
"Yes, well done. I never knew you were familiar with poisons."
"Well, everyone knows that, don't they? It is from all those spy stories we read as kids."

Sebastien lifts his head and rises to his feet.

"Cyanide is a fast-acting poison. It acts within seconds to minutes of ingestion. Therefore, she must have had the poison only minutes before she died."

"Well, clearly. She had the drink, and not long after, she started choking, as we saw."

Sebastien turned and looked around the room.

"Okay, let's set the scene."

He turns quickly and strides back towards the left corner of the room. Towards the left corner of the wall containing the door. He then turns to Archie.

"So, this was where we stood. You, me and Samantha. We stood here, Correct?"

"Yes, that is about the right place."

"Then to the right."

Sebastien pointed to the right corner opposite, again by the wall with the door.

"Was your Uncle Tony, Aunt Imogen, and Richard? Do you agree?

Archie moved to the right corner. He stood there, looking around him and then at the floor. "Yes, they were standing here.

"Good."

Sebastien then twisted, facing the centre of the room in the direction of the body. "Then, finally, in the centre of the room was the rest of our party."

"Yes," Archie replied. "There was Jessica, Kate, Rebecca,

Luke, and Daniel. They were all there in a huddle. Busy chatting"

"Yes, they were. They were all distracted."

Sebastien says. Quickly, he moves to the left side of the room as if he is against the left wall. Once in place, he then turns to the right, facing the central space.

"So, as we have said, we were standing with Samantha over there."

Sebastien says, pointing to the right corner.

"Your Uncle Tony, Aunt Imogen, and Richard were all standing over there."

He moves his hand to point to the left corner.

"And the rest, including Jessica, were all here."

He points to the middle.

"In the centre of the room."

"Yes, Okay."

Archie agrees.

"So, just before the murder happens, we are over there."

Again, he points to the right corner.

"Distracted with a conversation about disgusting food."

Archie raises his eyebrows, clearly not agreeing with this opinion.

"Your uncle's group was over there."

Sebastien continues, pointing to the left corner.

"Discussing something, and so they were distracted as well."

Sebastien turns to the centre of the room.

"And here we have the main group of interest. They are all here. Huddled around. Chatting. You agree with me so far?"

"Yes. Everything you have said makes sense to me."

"Great. So we agreed on where everyone was. Now to the waiter."

"The waiter? What waiter?"

"Don't you remember? The waiter that nearly spilled his tray?"

"Oh, that's right. What about him?"

"Okay, let's start from the beginning. The waiter enters the room. He goes around to the right. I presume he passes your uncle's group in the right corner. Whether or not any of them took a drink, we do not know. He then goes to the centre of the room. This is what I glimpsed when we were talking. He goes to the group containing Jessica. He offers them drinks. Jessica declines at first. As the waiter moves away, she changes her mind. She takes a glass from the tray while his head is turned. This causes him to lose the balance of the tray, nearly causing him to drop it to the floor."

"Oh yes. That is what we saw."

"Exactly. He then regains control of the tray and leaves."

"Perhaps he did it?"

Archie suggests enthusiastically.

"Perhaps he poisons the glass for her to drink?"

"No, Archie. I do not think so. Think it through. First, he would have had to be certain of which glass she would select. There is no way of knowing that. It may be more likely that she would select the glass closest to her, but it is not certain. He could only be certain if he offered a glass that he chose to her, which he did not. Secondly, how would he ensure that she would be the first person to get that glass? The answer is he cannot, especially as he goes to another group of people first. And thirdly, he did not know she even went for that glass. As we saw, he nearly dropped the tray because his head was turned, and so he did not know she was reaching for the glass. No, it is not possible that the waiter could have been our poisoner."

"Okay."

Replies Archie, a little deflated.

"So where does that leave us?"

"It means we know one thing."

"Which is?"

"That the glass could not have been poisoned before Jessica took it. Just as it was true for the waiter, it was true for everybody else. They could not have known which glass she would select. So, if they wanted to poison her, they would need to have waited for her to choose her glass first. Therefore, the glass must have been poisoned only after she had received it."

"Well, if that is the case, it must have been one of the other members of the group."

Archie suggests.

"Exactly. Samantha, you and I could not have done it as we were over there to the left. Similarly, neither could have Tony, Imogen, or Richard, as they were to the right. The only people who were close enough to Jessica to be able to poison her glass once she had it were Kate, Rebecca, Luke, and Daniel. So, it stands to reason that it must be one of them."

"But how? Surely, one of them would have noticed somebody putting cyanide into her glass. And why? Why would one of them want to kill her?"

"Well, is it really that hard to see how it could have happened? We saw them. They all stood around in a circle. Close together. They stood with their hands holding their glasses in front of them as you would naturally expect. Their glasses are all together at the centre. And then there is their discussion. As we saw, they were distracted. They were engaged and absorbed. They were focused on what was being said and switched their focus from one member of the group to another as the conversation flowed—not looking at what was going on in front of them and not looking beneath them. As their eye line was directed towards the face of the speaker. How easy would it be for one of them to discreetly pour some liquid into Jessica's glass when no one was looking? No. It is not hard to believe that one of them could have poisoned her glass without the others noticing. Not in that situation. As for your second question."

Sebastien shrugged.

"Well, we cannot answer that yet. It was clear that somebody did. One of them must have a motive. A reason that would drive them to kill her. That is if we are seeing this the right way in the first place."

"If we are seeing it the right way?"

Archie asked, confused.

"What do you mean? We saw her drink from a glass that could only have been poisoned after she had selected it. How can we be seeing this wrong?"

Sebastien nodded.

"Okay. Look at it this way. Who in that group would you think is most likely to be murdered? Who has the most enemies? The most people with a motive to kill them?"

Archie thinks for a second. His brow creased. "Well, Rebecca, I suppose. From what I heard earlier, Kate, Luke and Daniel could all have motives for her. Luke, in particular, sounded as if he could kill her when they argued. But this still does not change the fact that they poisoned Jessica's glass after she had chosen it. She had it in her hand. How could they have got the wrong one?"

"Yes. Exactly," Says Sebastien. Smiling at his friend. "Rebecca is the one you would suspect. From what we know, Luke, Kate and Daniel all have potential motives for her murder. But as you said, Jessica's glass was poisoned. How could they have got the wrong one? Well, let's think it through. Who was standing next to Rebecca?"

Archie sighs. He could kick himself. "Jessica," He says.

"Yes. Jessica is standing next to Rebecca. So, what if they accidentally put it in her glass instead? It may seem unlikely, but consider it for a moment. They are chatting and looking at each other's faces. Not their hands. The murderer has to remain focused on the conversation. They would have to act naturally. To move their eyes down to their hands would raise suspicion. Especially once the murder has taken place and the others think back more critically. So, they must keep their eyes level. Focused on whoever is talking. They cannot look below at what they are doing. They must work out where Rebecca's glass is by using where they can see she is standing. They must do this while remaining engaged in the conversation, contributing, and replying to any questions. Remember, they must not be suspicious. So, they put the poison in a glass in the direction of Rebecca. Is it not possible that in the midst of all of these other factors? All of these distractions and complications. That they could get the wrong glass. One that is so close by. Yes, it is completely possible. So, we must consider the possibility that Jessica was not the intended victim. That, in fact, it was Rebecca."

"God," Said Archie in shock.

"Although," Sebastien added. "We cannot, of course,

discount the possibility that Jessica was the intended victim. Only consider the possibility that Rebecca was. It means we must consider the motives the members of that group had for both the murder of Jessica and the potential murder of Rebecca."

Archie exhaled deeply. His hands were on his hips. "Well. So, we basically have to investigate two murders rather than one?" He said.

Sebastien turned to him. He shrugged. "Pretty much."

Archie nodded. Taking it all in. "Oh god", he said. A thought just came to him. "If Rebecca was the intended target. That means she is still in danger."

Sebastien pauses and then nods vigorously. "Yes, it does. We must find her and warn her."

CHAPTER 21

After the scene in the lounge, Rebecca decided to get a drink of water from the kitchen. She was still in shock. Jessica dead. On her birthday. Her choking and fitting in the middle of the party. It was just unbelievable. Unimaginable. How could this happen?

Walking to her room from the kitchen, she wondered what would happen next. What would this do to her mother? Her family? Would they ever be able to get over this? Would they ever be the same again?

As she neared the stairs, she saw Kate coming down the corridor towards her. In truth, she did not really register it. She had much more important thoughts on her mind.

As Kate comes closer to her. She says, "We need to talk. Come on," Grabbing her arm.

"What now?" Rebecca protests. "Really, can't it wait?"

"No," Kate says sternly. "It definitely cannot." Pulling her into a side room and shutting the door behind them.

Kate turns round to Rebecca, waiting expectantly. Keen to get this all over with. She just wants to go to bed.

"Why did you do it?" Kate asks. Her eyes pierced into Rebecca.

"Do what?"

Kate raised her eyebrows, widened her eyes and creased her forehead as if it was obvious what she was asking. "Why did you do it?" She spat out. "Why did you kill her?"

Rebecca was astounded. "What? Me? What do you mean, why did I kill her? I did not kill her."

"Come on. You are the only person there capable of murder. You are capable of anything. Why did you do it? What had she ever done to you? Did she threaten you in some way? Did she know some secrets of yours? Or was it just for your dad?"

"This is about us, isn't it?" Rebecca challenged. Infuriated by Kate's accusations. "This is about you and me. Not Jessica. You cannot just blame me for everything. All the problems in your life are not my fault. They are not of my making. It was your fault; what happened? It was your stupidity, naivety, error of judgment. Whatever you want to call it. The point is I did what I had to do. It was not my fault then, and this is not my fault now."

Kate scoffed. "Not your fault. You framed me. Cheated me. You cost me my career. It was all untrue, and you knew it was. You made it all up. So you could win."

Rebecca sighed. "Just tell yourself what you like. I know the truth, and one day you will hopefully accept it."

"Accept it? Accept your lies. Never. Do not try to gaslight me into thinking that I am wrong. That it is really my fault. I do know the truth. The truth is that you will do anything to get what you want. The question is, why was poisoning Jessica something you decided you had to do? Was it for your dad? Or was it because of something else?"

"My dad?" Rebecca says suspiciously. Does she know? Rebecca thought. Does she know about the firm's troubles? Is that why she suspects me? Suspects us?

Kate sees the suspicion in Rebecca's face. Her eyes moved rapidly. Her mouth hung open at the end of her speech. She sees her mind working. Calculating. God. Kate thinks. She knows. She knows about me and her father. Does that mean she did it? Did she poison Jessica to protect her father? Did he get her to do it? Was all that stuff earlier planned to manipulate me after he got his daughter to do his dirty work? Or did she do it by herself? Did she find out about us, or did he tell her? Did she then decide to protect her family by killing my friend? Kate does not know what to think. This is too much. She has too many thoughts going through her head. Horrible thoughts. It isn't very good. Jessica is killed by her own family. Is it the truth, though? Would they even go that far? Well, Rebecca might. She has shown herself to be truly selfish and completely remorseless. If anyone could do it, she could.

"This is ridiculous," Rebecca shouted. Trying to regain control. "I did not kill her. I did not murder my cousin. It is just absolutely insane." She paused for a moment. She then fixed Kate with a stare. "Why are you so sure it is me? Why are you so certain? Pulling me in here? Throwing all these accusations? Perhaps it is because you do not believe any of them? Perhaps all this is. This posturing. This ranting. Is all about diverting suspicion away from you."

"What?"

"You heard me. I think you are doing all of this to deflect suspicion onto me. Away from yourself."

"That is rubbish. It is completely and utterly ridiculous. Why would I ever want to hurt Jess? Let alone kill her?"

Rebecca shrugged. "I don't know. Maybe you had a falling out. Maybe you met in London without anyone knowing, and it happened. Or maybe she knew a secret. One you could not bear to come out. Who knows?"

"This is complete nonsense. I would never hurt Jess. Never. And for the record, I have no reason to kill her. No argument. No sordid secret. Nothing. If it were you, then it would be another matter. But Jess. No. I would not kill her."

"Oh, so you would kill me."

"After what you did. What have you done to me and the others? It would be all that you deserve."

Rebecca threw up her hands. "Christ. You are mad. I am not putting up with this any longer."

With that, she turned, opened the door, strode through it, and slammed it behind her.

CHAPTER 22

God, that girl is insane. Rebecca thinks as she walks away. She is just hysterical. Completely irrational. Just forcing me into that room and then standing there accusing me of murder and shouting and screaming in my face. She is just mad. She thinks I would kill my cousin. Why? Why would I do it? What possible reason could I have? The answer, of course, is none. I have no reason to want her dead. Kate knows that. She just wants it to be me, and therefore, in her mind, it must be me. There is also the other point I made. By accusing me, she moves the blame onto me and away from herself. Could she have killed her? Why? Was I right? Did they have some argument in London? Is there some secret that Jessica was about to reveal? Are either of these things enough to make Kate kill her?

Walking down the corridor to the stairs, Rebecca does not

know. How can she? It has all been so quick. So brutal. She has barely had time to think. Has it even really sunk in yet? That her cousin is dead? That Jess is gone. She does not know. Perhaps once she gets to her room, she will just collapse in a heap on the floor. Weeping her eyes out. Or maybe she will just become a drone. Going through the motions. Desperate to escape into her sleep.

"Rebecca!"

She turns round. Sees Archie and that friend of his are rushing towards her.

Not now. She thinks. I am really not in the mood for this now.

"Rebecca," Archie says, slightly out of breath. "We need to..."

"No," She interrupts. "I really do not want to do this now. Actually, I cannot. I cannot talk and chat. I cannot be all friendly and polite now. I have had enough. What I need to do is go to bed."

"Please," Sebastien says softly. "We understand how difficult today has been for you, especially you, but this is important for your safety and Jessica. Just give us a few minutes, please."

Rebecca eyed him up for a moment. Unsure what she made of him. After a pause, she said. "Ok, fine. I am walking back to my room. You can talk to me until I get there. But that is it."

"Thank you," Sebastien replied gratefully.

They started walking slowly towards the staircase. Sebastien is on the left. Rebecca is in the middle. And Archie on the right.

"Can you think of any reason someone would want to kill your cousin?" Sebastien asked. His tone is soft and light. But also respectful.

"No," She replied, sighing. "I can't. She was a twenty-year-old fashion student. Why would anyone want to kill her?"

"She had no disagreements with anyone. No fights? No rivalries? You cannot think of any enemies?"

"No," Rebecca said with a small laugh. "Jessica was the most easy-going person I knew. She was not the type to have disagreements or fights. Or to develop rivalries either. I certainly cannot see her developing any enemies. As I said, it just does not make sense."

Sebastien nodded. Considering this. "Would you say the same thing about yourself?"

"What do you mean?"

"Well, would you say that you are the type of person who does not have disagreements or fights? To develop rivalries. To have enemies?"

After a pause, she replied. "Me and Jessica were different people. I am ambitious and determined. She was not. The fact is that any ambitious young woman is likely to be considered the type you suggested."

"But is this how you think of yourself?"

Rebecca stopped and turned to him. "What has this got to do with Jessica's death? Surely, you should be asking more about her. Rather than focusing your attention on me."

"Well, to understand what can happen between two people, you must first consider both of those people. But particularly in this case, there is a reason we are so interested in you."

Rebecca looked puzzled.

"We think you are in danger, Rebecca," Archie said. "We think they wanted to poison you."

She laughed. "What?" She looked between them. "You cannot be serious."

"I can assure you, we most certainly are," Sebastien said seriously.

"Me? Why would anyone want to kill me? And how could I be the target? They poisoned her drink. It just does not make sense."

"Does it not?" Sebastien replied. "You two are standing next to each other. At a busy drinks party. Is it not possible the murderer selected the wrong glass?"

"Well, maybe it could happen. Theoretically. But, who would want to kill me?"

"Did you not just say that you are the type of person to have disagreements, make rivalries and have enemies?"

Rebecca scoffed. "That does not mean people want to murder me. Listen, I am a strong, outspoken woman. Naturally, that means I sometimes clash with people. But that does not mean they want to poison me. There is nothing in my life that would cause someone to want me dead."

"Unfortunately, it tends to be the murderer, not the victim, who decides what is worth killing for. Something that may seem trivial to you could be the most important thing in the world to them. It is all about perspective."

Rebecca rolled her eyes. Continuing to walk up the stairs.

"Is there anyone here tonight who could wish you harm?"

Rebecca was silent for a moment. Thinking.

"No," She finally replied. Her head held high.

"No one that you have disagreed with? No one who feels angry with you?"

"No," Rebecca replied instantly.

Sebastien shrugs. "Very well, if you are sure. But if you do have the slighted feeling that someone here may bear a grudge against you. I would advise you to say now."

Rebecca sighs. "No, there is no one here who has a grudge against me. Okay?"

"Okay," Sebastien accepts reluctantly. "I just wanted to be sure."

They walk in silence for a few moments.

"Wait a minute," Rebecca says. "To understand what can happen between two people. You think I did it?" She said, shocked.

"Not necessarily," Sebastien replied. "Just that you are one of the people with the opportunity to do so. But did you have any disagreements with your cousin? Any problems?"

"No," Rebecca replied rapidly. "We did not have any problems. We never do. We get along well. Well, we got along. And we had not seen each other for months before this weekend. How could we?"

"Were there any problems in the family? Any rifts? Anything which divided you?"

"No," Rebecca said anxiously. "There is nothing going on

in our family. There are no rifts or divisions. It is all just normal... well, it was before all this." Turning to her right, she said, "And this is where I leave you," indicating the door of her bedroom.

"Of course, you have been most helpful. But could we ask you just one more thing? Then I promise we will leave you in peace."

Rebecca sighed. She really did just want to sleep. Nothing else, just sleep. Just to get away from all this. But at least once this was done, they would leave.

"Fine. One last thing," She said.

"Thank you. Did you notice anything suspicious in the minutes leading up to Jessica's death? Anything at all?"

Rebbeca shook her head, side to side. "Nope, nothing." Without saying goodbye. She opened her door. Immediately entering and slamming it behind her.

Sebastien and Archie looked at each other.

"Well," Archie said. "At least she was pleased to see us."

"Well, what could we expect? It has been a tough day. But at least we learned something."

"Did we learn something?"

"Of course we did. We learned that she lies. She lied to us about anyone in this house having a motive to harm her. Well, from their argument earlier, it was clear to see that Luke did. It was also implied that Kate and Daniel did as well. Yes, this was something she would know, and yet she chose to lie about it to us. Why?"

Archie thought. "Because she was guilty?"

"Maybe. Or maybe because she knew she had lied. Betraying her friends to benefit herself. And now she is afraid of these lies being exposed. But either way, she lied. The real question is, what else is she lying about?"

CHAPTER 23

As they are coming down the stairs. After their interview with Rebecca. Sebastien and Archie are still debating what to think.

"Do you think she was the target then? The intended victim?"

Sebastien sighed. "Archie. I do not know. All that we know is that it is completely realistic to assume that she could have been the intended victim. Whether or not she was, we cannot say yet. I mean, she clearly thinks she was not. When we spoke to her, it was clear that she was not afraid."

As they reached the bottom of the stairs. They walked down the corridor. As they moved further, they started to hear a sound—heavy breathing. Someone crying.

Slowing down, Sebastien heard that the noise was coming from a room to the left. Looking at Archie, He cocked his head in the direction of the room. This indicates that something was wrong and that they should see what was happening. Archie nodded in agreement.

They opened the door and found Kate. She sat against the wall. Her knees were drawn close to her. Her arms wrapped around them in a hug. Crying heavily with her head buried into them.

Sebastien crouched down on his tiptoes. "Excuse me, are you alright?" He asked.

Kate looked up. Startled. She quickly straightened her legs and wiped her face. Her distress was still clear to see from the redness and puffiness of her cheeks.

"Yes," She said with a small laugh. Her face going a little more red. Clearly embarrassed at being caught. "It is just today. Everything that has happened. It is just all so horrible. Poor, poor Jess. I just cannot believe it is happening."

Sebastien nodded sympathetically. "Yes, today has certainly not been what any of us expected. It has been terrible, as you say. Especially, I fear, for you. I gather you were particularly close to Jess. Do you mind if we?" He gestured to the space to her side.

"Oh yes, go ahead."

Sebastien sat against the wall on her right side. Archie

then took the space to her left. With his knees bent, Sebastien turned himself to her.

"So, you were close to her?" He asked. His tone is incredibly soft and gentle.

"Yes, we have been best friends since school. I lived nearby and was always coming to Claytons. We would spend hours listening to music and gossiping in her room or lying on the grass gazing at the clouds. And we would play pranks. Oh, how she loved to play pranks. It was great. If only I could go back." She said this with longing. Looking absently into the space in front of her. Her mind was distracted with more pleasant times.

"Yes," Sebastien replied. " And so, you are familiar with the family then? Her aunt and uncle?" Carefully bringing her back to the moment.

Kate hesitated. "Yes. Imogen is lovely. She is a little stiff. But she has been welcoming me in since I was little."

"And Tony?"

"Oh, him? Well, he wasn't around much," She replied dismissively.

Sebastien nodded with a thin smile. "And recently," Sebastien said. "Had you seen much of Jess before this weekend?"

Kate stared down and bit her lip. "To be honest, I haven't. I have barely seen her in ages. We just have such different lives. Her with her studying and me with my work. And even though we both live in London. We are in completely different areas. We just never got round to seeing each other."

"I understand," Sebastien said. "Life has a way of separating us all. What is it that you do?"

"I work in a cafe in Islington. It is a nice place. They are good to work for, and the pay is decent. I have made so many new friends."

"That is excellent," said Sebastien, smiling. "I am just curious, though. Did you never consider university? It is just the rest of your childhood friends are students, from what I can gather. I just wondered."

For a moment, Kate became slightly tense. Taking a moment to reply. But she then seemed to relax and said. "I did think about it but decided that it was not for me. It isn't for everyone. And it is not the only way to success." She smiled confidently at him.

"No, of course," He said with a smile. "What you do is very commendable. To move to a new city, far from home and build a life for yourself. That is truly an achievement."

She smiled brightly. Accepting his praise.

"Unfortunately, I must ask you some questions which you may not like," Sebastien said. His smile was replaced with a serious look. "Would you be willing to answer them?"

Kate's smile turned into a look of caution as if she was wary of him. Not sure what she should expect. "If it helps with all this, please go ahead."

Sebastien nods. "Is there any reason you can think of why someone would want to harm Jess?"

"No," She said passionately. "No reason at all. She was the most wonderful, kind-hearted, funny girl I know. There isn't any reason why someone would want to kill her?"

"Unfortunately, it appears that someone found one," Sebastien remarked. "Did you notice anything in the minutes leading up to her death? Anyone else acting strangely?"

She flinched. The memory of that time, and even just hearing the words, is an unpleasant experience. "I do not think so." She replied. Her brow creased, in thought. "We were all just talking. It was all going great. We were laughing and chatting away. I can't remember what we were talking about. But it was all friendly. I think the drink helped a bit with that."

Sebastien gave a small smile. Understanding what she meant.

"And what about Rebecca?"

Again, she became tense. She was frowning and sighed. "What about her?" She said in a harsh tone.

"Well, can you think of any reason why someone would want to harm her?"

Kate gave a small laugh. "I can think of several. She was someone who had no trouble stepping over others to get what she wanted." Stopping herself, she said, "What has this got to do with Jess?"

Sebastien cocked his head to one side. "Only that she may not have been the intended victim. It may have been Rebecca who they intended to poison."

"Oh," Kate said. Shocked by the thought. "That is awful, obviously." Although, she said this pleasantly enough. It still lacked the feeling that it was genuine.

"So, can you think of any reasons?" Sebastien pressed.

Kate looked at him in the eye. "No. Rebecca could be a difficult person, but nobody would want to kill her."

"Would they not? You just said yourself that she was happy to trample over others to get what she wanted. That sounds very much to me like someone who others could want to kill." After a pause, Sebastien asked. "Is one of those people you?"

Kate's face developed a look of anxiety. "No. No, of course not," She said rapidly. Her voice became faster and higher pitched as her anxiety took hold. "I don't want to kill Rebecca. No, of course I don't. Why would you say that? It is absolutely untrue." Her voice became a shout towards the end.

Sebastien put up his hands. "Please, calm yourself. I meant no offence," He said gently. "I do not think that you do. I just needed to ask. You see, I heard something earlier said about you and Rebecca. I could not quite catch it. But it was something about how she cheated you. Betrayed you, perhaps?"

Kate paused for a moment. Her breathing was still deep but was now getting calmer. Her mind was busy—a look of distraction on her face.

"Oh, that," She said with a small laugh. Her smile returned. "Oh, that was nothing. We just had a small disagreement. You see, we were planning to go to see a concert. We both said we wanted to go. Anyway, Rebecca managed to get her ticket first and found out there was only one other left. She decided to get it for her boyfriend rather than me. Naturally, I was upset at the time. I did feel cheated and betrayed about it then. But that was all in the past. All forgotten now."

Quickly rising to her feet, Kate said. "You know, I just feel so tired. I am going to go to bed. You don't mind, do you?"

She asked, looking at both of us. We had both now risen as well.

"No, not at all," Sebastien said casually and with a friendly smile. "Please do not let us keep you."

"See you later then," Kate replied. With a wave. Going out the door.

Archie looked to Sebastien. "So, what do you think?" He asked.

"I think that she is lying."

"Really? I wasn't sure if she was, to be honest."

"No. I am certain of it. She is lying. Her initial response to our question about reasons to harm Rebecca. It was instinctive, natural before she caught herself. No. A disagreement over a concert ticket would not induce such an instinct. It would be forgotten by now. And her reaction to the question of whether she could be such a person to want to hurt her. It resulted in a passionate, desperate denial. It was full of anxiety. Clearly, she felt that she had a reason to be afraid. No. She must be lying. Rebecca's action must have been something that had a greater impact than she had made out. And then there is the fact that she did not go to university."

Archie looked puzzled. "What about it? You said it was a good thing."

" Well, I did not exactly say that. I agree that university is not the only path, and what she has achieved is remarkable. What concerns me is why. I do not believe it was her choice not to go."

"So, you think she was rejected? Why? Does it have something to do with Rebecca?"

"That we do not know. All we know is that she became tense when asked about why she did not go to university—

indicating that it was something that she felt uncomfortable about. This implies that it was not her choice, as she claimed. So, it could do. Something that would affect her getting into her chosen university may explain the response we saw." Sebastien paused. "The question is, would it be enough to kill over?"

CHAPTER 24

Having left the room where they spoke to Kate. Sebastien and Archie were now walking towards the stairs.

They walked up towards the door of the lounge. Which they can see is open. As they do so, they notice a figure hunched in one of the armchairs by the fire. Drinking a yellow-coloured liquid out of a tumbler. It's probably a whisky of some sort.

Veering off, Sebastien decides to enter the room. With Archie soon following.

As they make their way around, they see it is Daniel. Curled into the armchair. Clutching his drink. His eyes fixed on the fire. Examining the flames and crackles it creates. Sebastien thinks such a pastime might be quite mindful. Just focusing on this creation of nature. Everything else is driven out of your mind.

Sebastien takes a seat on the sofa in the corner closest to Daniel. Archie then takes a seat to his right. Daniel has not realized yet that either of them is there. The fire just absorbs him.

"It has been an awful day, hasn't it?" Sebastien says. Matter of fact. Trying to break the ice.

Daniel is slightly startled for a moment. Unaware that anyone had entered the room. He turns his head and sees them both. He looks them both up and down. He then turns back to the fire in a rather dismissive fashion. "Yes, it has. " He replies bluntly. Clearly not interested in talking.

"You knew Jessica since you were children, I believe?" Sebastien persisted.

"Yes"

"And is there any reason that you can think of why anyone would want to hurt her?"

Daniel turned his head and looked Sebastien straight in the eye. "What is it to you?"

Sebastien shrugged. "Nothing, really. It is just such a terrible thing; I was just trying to make sense of it." He paused before adding. "So do you?"

Daniel looked at him for a second longer before returning to the fire. "No," He barked before taking another sip of his drink.

"Really? Is there nothing at all you can think of? Any reason why someone would want her dead?"

Not moving, Daniel replied. "Jess didn't upset people.

Everyone who knew her liked her. No one would want to kill her."

"Okay. What about Rebecca, then?"

Daniel gritted his teeth. "What about her?" He snarled before taking a swig from his glass.

"Is there any reason why someone would want to harm her? To kill her?"

"Oh, I think the better question is, who wouldn't want to kill her? That toxic bitch" Having realized he had spoken his thoughts out loud, Daniel said. "A joke." A large, somewhat sinister smile appeared on his face. Wholly unconvincing. "She is a... trying person, but no one would kill her for that?

"Trying how?" Sebastien asked.

Daniel turned to him momentarily. "Just is," He said as if he was spelling out the words to an idiot.

"Really? So, she never, shall we say, cheated you?" Sebastien looked straight into Daniels's eyes.

Daniel turned. Angling himself so he could lean over the edge of his chair and face Sebastien directly. His eyes drilled into him.

With the same menacing smile, Daniel said. "What would possibly give you that idea?" His voice took a sinister edge.

"Oh, I just heard something somewhere," Sebastien replied, unnerved. "That she had cheated you. Betrayed you. So, did she?"

Daniel was silent for a few seconds. That menacing grin fixed on his face. Directed at Sebastien. Until he said. "No. I think you have been misinformed. Over the years, we have had our disagreements. Who doesn't? But I wouldn't say she has ever cheated me. I don't know where you could have got that from."

Sebastien stared at him for a moment. His face is serious. Before smiling. "Of course," He says cheerfully. "I must have been mistaken."

Daniel looks at both of them before finishing his drink and then putting it on the side table next to him. He then rises from his chair and says, "Night." His characteristic grin plastered across his face. Without another word, he makes for the door and leaves the room.

Archie looks to Sebastien. "Did we really need to talk to that prick?"

Sebastien nods. "What he had to tell us was very useful. Despite the fact that he was, indeed, a prick."

"So, what was it that was useful? As far as I could see, he said nothing much of use at all."

"On the contrary. He showed us that we were right. That he did have a motive to kill Rebecca. She had cheated him."

"He denied that. "

Sebastien made a skeptical look. "Yes, but not very well. His original response was, like Kate's, instinctive. Before he consciously thought about what he was saying. It showed us his true feelings. Hatred and anger. Why? Because she had cheated him in some way. We just do not yet know how."

"And Jessica? What about her?"

Sebastien sighed. "That was a little less informative. He may have a motive, or he may not. That we could not see."

Archie awned. "God, this is all making my head hurt. I think I could literally just sleep here if I let myself. I am that tired."

Sebastien did not look at him. His focus was drawn to the fire. The flames were dying now. A glowing pile of embers emerges. Sitting on this pile was a grey sheet. Burnt by the flames. It was thin and looked like a piece of burnt cloth. Charred by the fire, it had become curled and misshapen.

Carefully reaching into the fire, Sebastien lightly picks the fabric up. Being careful not to damage it or burn himself.

"What do you make of this?" He asked.

Archie stared at it for a second. "Don't know, really. Is it some card or something?"

Sebastien examined the material. Turning it over in his hand. "No. It looks more like it was a piece of cloth. Fabric. Like a handkerchief."

"Ok, so what?" Archie said. Losing interest in the topic.

"So why was it in the fire? Who decided to burn it?"

Archie shrugged. "Maybe it was dirty, so they threw it away."

"But it is fabric. Why not just wash it? Why waste it by burning it?"

"Oh, I don't know, Seb, it is not important."

"Maybe. Or maybe we just don't know its importance yet," Getting a clean tissue out of his pocket. Sebastien wrapped the burnt remains in it and put it into his jacket pocket."

Archie sighs. "Alright. You happy now?"

"No" Sebastien murmurs. "Not with all these loose ends, I am not. All the answers we have found just result in new questions. No, I am not happy at all."

"God. You are such a drama queen. Come on. Let's go to

bed. I'm knackered, and so are you. We can come back to this in the morning."

Sebastien nodded reluctantly. "Yes, okay. Best have a good night's... wait a second. I am not a drama queen."

"You are"

"Are not"

Archie sighed. "Let's just continue this argument while we go up the stairs. You will have us here all night otherwise."

CHAPTER 25

Imogen and Tony were both exhausted. First, the whole business of entertaining. Being the hosts. Making sure everything was going as it should. That everyone was enjoying themselves. And then, what came next?

In their bedroom. They had both changed into their night-clothes. Imogen was sat at her dressing table. Looking into her mirror. As she removed her makeup, she was ready for bed. Tony was in their ensuite, cleaning his teeth.

Imogen had moved into a sort of automatic state. Carrying out the motions of the actions she did every night. She was not really thinking about what she was doing. Her mind was filled with thoughts of what they saw.

Jessica. Oh, poor Jessica. She thinks. It was so horrible.

Her struggling on the floor like that. Twisting and spasming. Choking. Until it just stopped. She stopped. A tear went down Imogen's cheek. Poor, poor girl. Why? Why did this happen to her? What had she ever done to deserve this? She was innocent—my dear, beautiful girl.

Wiping her face, her train of thought continues. How could this happen? On today of all days. It was just terrible. I don't know what I will do. Every moment, it feels like she will come through the door. This all being some mistake. Some horrible joke. It doesn't feel like this is real. How can it be? It just doesn't feel possible that she could now be dead. And what about what Samantha said? That she was poisoned, was that true? Had someone murdered her? Had they chosen that she should die? But why? Who would want to hurt Jessica? Let alone kill her. Imogen struggled to believe it. She was such a lovely girl. Full of energy and light. And now she was cold. She was gone.

As Tony came in from the bathroom, Imogen straightened herself. Taking a deep breath. He came over to her and put his hand on her shoulder. Looking at her face in the mirror. "How are you feeling?" He asked. His concern was clear in his voice.

She looked back at him—a look of calmness on her face. "I am okay." She said. "It is just so terrible. For it to happen. She was so young."

Tony nodded. He removed his hand and moved back in the direction of the bed. "Yes, it is such a tragedy." He said, getting into bed. "As you say, she was so young. Her life ahead of her. But I suppose we just have to carry on. Do the best we can."

Imogen nodded. Yes, he was right. There was no point wallowing. She would grieve Jessica. But life carried on. They would all, in time, feel their pain fade away.

"Besides, there is perhaps one small piece of good to come out of all this," Tony added.
Imogen turned round. Confused. "What do you mean?"
"Well, the inheritance. From her trust."

For a moment, Imogen was puzzled. Unsure of what he meant. Then it hit her. Of course, the trust. The one set up for Jessica when her parents died. It had not even occurred to Imogen. How could it? She did not want it. She wanted her niece back. How could it have occurred to him? So quickly? Jessica is barely cold, and he is thinking about what money we can get out of it. The idea made Imogen furious.

"It could be useful," He went on. "With all this stuff at the firm. That money could ensure that we can keep the house. I know what happened is terrible, but I am sure Jessica would not want us to miss an opportunity. I am just saying. There is a silver lining to everything."

Silver lining? My niece is dead. Her life was cut short. And he is talking about a silver lining. Of a horrific death. Imogen was preparing herself to respond. To attack. Getting ready for the row she intended to have. Then she thought of something.

Could Tony have been involved in it? Could he have had a part in Jessica's death? The thought filled Imogen with horror. No. she thought suddenly. No, he wouldn't do that. He couldn't. But it was strange. All this talk about money. Our inheritance. Could that have been the plan? A way out of the troubles he has caused for us. Imogen did not know. She did not know what to think. Everything she had thought about her life had been turned upside down today. She looked at him. Sat up in the bed. Ready to go to sleep. Could he have done it? Could he have killed her? My husband. The man I have shared my life with for over thirty years.

Imogen turned back to the mirror. She was feeling a mixture of emotions. Horror. Disgust. Fear. It was just unimaginable. How could this even be happening? This morning, all I had to worry about was whether the house was presentable and whether the food was up to standard. Now, I am considering if my husband could have killed my niece. It was just all too much. What am I going to do?

Okay, just calm down. She told herself. This is ridiculous. Tony wants to save the house, of course, but he would not kill Jessica. No. He just sees an opportunity—one which could save us. Enable us to keep the house we love. I love. It does not mean he killed her. No. He is just being practical. Rational. That is it. And how could he have done it anyway? He was in another part of the room with me when it happened. No. I am being ridiculous. I need to stop. Now more than ever, I need him.

Getting up. She moves across the room. To her side of the bed and under the covers. As Tony lifts his arm, she nestles into him. Secured in a hug. "It will be alright, my darling." He says, Kissing her on the head. "Everything will be alright. You'll see."

CHAPTER 26

A foul mood overcame the house the morning after. They were sat in the dining room. Helping themselves to a buffet laid out on a side table against the wall. Croissants, muffins, eggs, sausages. Then, returning to the long dining table that ran down the centre of the room.

There was no discussion today. None of the polite small talk you would have about your plans for the day ahead. Everyone was silent. Wrapped up in their thoughts. The events of last night are still raw.

When Sebastien came down, there were five other people in the room. Tony was sitting at the head of the table. His head was buried in the paper. Imogen was sitting on his right. Drinking tea and slowly making her way through her food. Three seats down from her was Kate. She appeared to have started eating her breakfast. Before deciding, she was finished. Her cutlery is positioned upright in the middle of her plate. She was now staring straight ahead. A look of great sadness on her face. Her mind was consumed with thoughts. Whether they were longing for happier times or dwelling on the horrors of the night before was unknown. Two seats down from her was Daniel. He was ploughing through a hearty breakfast and only stopping to check his phone and acting as if everything was normal. Then, Archie was on the other side of the table. He was eating his breakfast slower than he normally would, clearly affected by the atmosphere in the room.

After a moment, he saw me. He made a small smile and nodded. Anything greater could have been rude in this house of the morning. He cocked his head to the right, towards the breakfast buffet. Indicating I should get some food. Although, it felt wrong to eat anything in this place where everyone was so depressed. Where they were still in mourning, I was also starving. Missing dinner the night before had caused a strong hunger. Deciding it was for the best, I went to the side and selected some eggs and bacon, which I put on a plate.

As I was doing this, Richard entered the room. Noticing he had come in alone, Imogen asked, "Where is Samantha? Is everything alright?" There was concern in her voice. I suppose the events of the previous night made her worry more about the loved ones she had left.

"Yes, everything is fine," Richard replied with a small smile. "She is just feeling a bit sick, that is all. Nothing to worry about. She said she may get up later if she feels better. I am just going to have something to eat, and then I will go back to her."

Imogen gave a rapid nod after being reassured. Tony glanced at her with a reassuring smile. He then put a supportive hand on top of hers.

As Richard came over to get some breakfast, I left to return to the table. Going past each other, we each gave a subtle nod in recognition. I then went and sat in the seat next to Archie.

"It has been like this for the last twenty minutes." He whispered. Taking care that no one else could hear. "It is almost unbearable."

"I guess everyone is still coming to terms with what happened," I replied. "Considering how close we all were to the event, I cannot blame them."

After a few seconds, two men entered the room. The first one was lean with brown hair. Slightly shorter than his companion. The second was more muscular with dark black hair. They are both dressed in suits and ties. My guess was they were police officers, which was soon proved correct.

"Excuse me, ladies and gentlemen." The first said. "Thank you for your co-operation. We understand that this is a difficult time for you all. I think we have spoken to most of you. I think their are; however, still, some of you from whom we need to get statements."

He surveyed the room, landing on me and Archie. "You

two," He said. Looking at us. I was already looking at him, having turned when I first heard his voice. Archie was still making his way through his meal and only realized once I gave him a nudge. "Us?" I checked.

"Yes," He confirmed. "We have not spoken before. You are?"

"Sebastien. Sebastien Blake," I said, pointing to myself. "And Archie. Archie Kingsley." He smiled and gave a brief nod.

"Ah yes, the cousin and the friend."

"Yes, that's us," I replied.

The man nodded. "Well, why don't you come with me to give your statement, and your friend can go with my sergeant?"

I made a swift glance towards my plate. I was starving. But this would get it over with. It was inevitable, anyway.

"Yes, of course," I agreed. Rising from my chair. Archie looked at me as if I had agreed to us taking an ice bath. To be honest, I am not sure which option would be worse.

Leaving the room with these men. The one who had addressed me said, "This way." At the same time, Archie was guided in the opposite direction. I followed him through the corridor and into the lounge where we had found Daniel the previous evening. He gestured to the sofa and told me to sit while he sat in the armchair nearby.

"I'm sorry," I said. "But I don't think you told me your name."

"Richards. Inspector Richards"

"Well, Inspector, how can I help you?"

He paused for a moment. "You can start by telling me why you are here?" He said. It was pleasant enough, but it had a clear undertone to it.

"It is simple, really. My friend does not see this part of his family much. He thought he would be lonely this weekend. So, he asked me to come to keep him company. And I was stupid enough to agree."

The Inspector nodded. Taking the information in. "Very well. Had you met Jessica before this weekend?"

"No, never. The first I met her was coming down the stairs to the party. The first I had heard of her was yesterday evening."

"And the rest of the family, were you familiar with them?"

"No. Again, this is the first time I have met them. I am just a plus one."

"Just a plus one?" The inspector let that linger there for a moment. "When you spoke to Jessica on the stairs. How did she seem?"

"She seemed fine. Happy even. Which, according to Archie, is how she usually was."

"And the rest of the family? How did they seem in the run-up to the party?"

"They seemed normal. I only met her aunt and uncle briefly when I arrived before going to my room. Nothing seemed out of the ordinary about them. Just two hosts welcoming guests and reuniting with family. I spoke to her cousin, Samantha, going up the stairs. She was normal. We just made small talk. I only met her other cousin, Rebecca, at the party briefly. I just said hello to her, really. So, I can't really say much about her."

"I understand. And her friends. What did you make of them?"

Sebastien sighed. "Well, not much, really. I only saw them at the party. I can't really say" Telling a white lie.

"Tell me honestly," The inspector said. Leaning in towards him. "As an outsider. What do you think? Who do you think did it?"

Sebastien paused for a few seconds. Thinking through his response. "Well, that depends," He said. "How did she die? Was it poison?"

The inspector nodded. "We suspect there are traces of Cyanide in her glass. Lab tests will confirm. So, what do you think?"

Sebastien sighed. "Well, if that is the case, it seems like only one of the four people she was with could have killed her. Only they would have had the opportunity."

"This being Rebecca, Kate, Daniel and Luke?" The inspector checked.

"Yes. Only they could have poisoned her glass as only they were close enough to her when she had it."

The inspector nodded. "And, of course, as she chose it randomly from a tray, it could not have been poisoned beforehand. If it was intended for her."

"Exactly," I agreed.

"So, any thoughts?"

"Honestly, inspector. I cannot think that any of them are any more likely to kill her than the rest. Sorry"

The inspector nodded, disappointed.

"Is there anything else, inspector?" I asked. Ready to rise from my chair.

"No, no," He replied absently. "Thank you for your time."

I then rose from my seat and began to walk towards the door.

"Actually," The inspector said. Causing me to stop and turn back around towards him. "Just one more thing. Where were you standing in the room when she died?"

"I was in the left corner of the room, by the wall containing the door. Both Archie and Samantha were with me. Until she started choking, at which point, like everyone else, we went to the centre of the room to see what was happening."

The inspector nodded. "Thank you for your time." He said.

"Not at all," I replied. Walking out of the room.

As I walked through the corridor, lots of thoughts went through my mind. Why did he want to know where I stood? Surely, he already knew this from what others had said. Did he suspect me? Did he think I did it? If so, how? I was nowhere near her when she received her glass. And did he believe my reason for being here? Did he believe that I did not know the family before? Did he believe anything I said?

Walking along the corridor, I was unsure. It was impossible to know what the detective had been thinking. But I was not worried. These questions would only worry me if I had killed her or had something else to hide. As I had neither, there was no reason to be concerned even if I did tell a tiny white lie.

Just then, Archie came round a corner up ahead. Smiling, he came towards me. "Glad I found you; how did it go?"

Sebastien shrugged. "It was okay. Nothing particularly important. He just asked about how the family were and what I was doing here. How about you?"

"Oh. He just asked me about what I saw at the party really and about the family. All seemed pretty straightforward. But it was nerve-wracking. I've never been interviewed by the police before. It feels as if they are trying to trip you up."

"They can only trip you up if you have something to be guilty of and, therefore, can be tripped up over."

Archie pondered this for a moment. "Yes, I guess you're right. Oh well, all over now."

"Did you tell him anything about us going to the murder scene and talking to her friends?"

"No. He did not ask. Did you?"

"No. He asked if I had any thoughts about any of them, and I said no."

Archie frowned at him.

"What?" Sebastien said.

"That is not strictly true, is it? You have done very little but have thoughts about them since she died."

"Ok. Yes. Perhaps I told a white lie from that perspective. But not from another. Even though our discussions with them have raised questions, they have not given us the answers. I still do not have any definitive thoughts on who did it—just various thoughts on who could have done it and why. To give them anything useful, we first must find the answers to our questions."

"And how do we do that?" Archie asked.

"We do that by speaking to the final member of that group. Luke. We must find him."

CHAPTER 27

After wandering around the house in their search for Luke, Sebastien and Archie were at a loss. They simply couldn't find him. Deciding that this meant he was outside, they searched the grounds. When that produced nothing, they then went on to explore the moor.

Moving through it now. Sebastien thought that it really was wild. Rough, uneven terrain. Covered in gorse and moss. Giant rocky boulders. Looking as if they have burst out of the earth. Yes, this was wild. Uncontrollable.

Sebastien hoped they found Luke soon. Moving across the uneven ground was a struggle. Making the entire exercise a tiring one. It was also very cold. He cursed himself for not bringing some thicker clothing. He was feeling the chill right down to the bone. No, he decided. If they did not find Luke soon, they would have to turn back. That is, if they could find their way back.

Just as he was starting to think it was hopeless and was just about to tell Archie that they should turn back, Sebastien saw a figure in the distance. Who it was, he could not tell. But from the hair, height and build, it could be Luke. That was good enough.

They picked up their pace, moving in his direction. As he was moving at a deliberately slow speed, it was not hard to catch up.

"Luke," Sebastien shouted when they were only a few steps behind.

The figure turned round. It was certainly Luke. But he did not look well. His face was pale, his eyes bruised as though he had not slept. But the worst thing was his expression. It was one of total despair, as if all the life had been sucked out. As if there was nothing he could care about anymore.

"It is good to see you," Sebastien said. "We were worried we would never find you."

Luke looked at them. His eyes were empty. "Why should I want to be found." He said. Turning round to complete his journey.

"Sometimes that is the time we most need finding," Sebastien replied gently. After a pause, he said. "Can I ask you something?"

Luke just shrugged. His eyes were not moving and just staring ahead.

"How long?" Sebastien asked.

"How long what?" Luke replied without interest.

"How long did you love her?"

Luke turned round suddenly, facing him. His eyes are starting to well up. His face started to tremble. "What are you talking about?" He screamed.

"Your response after her death. It was not that of just a friend. Even a close one. No. You were in absolute despair. You collapsed into a heap. Absolutely distraught. And then there was your response to Samantha's accusations. Your switch from your complete agony to the most passionate, most fierce display of defiance. That was love. You truly loved her. That is what I am talking about."

Luke stared him down for a moment before falling apart. He cried and lost his balance. Archie had to catch him as he fell. He buried himself into Archie, still crying. Archie put his arms around the man and then looked at Sebastien. His look meant, 'Now look what you have done; what the hell am I supposed to do now?'. Sebastien replied with another look. This meant, 'how should I know.' As his sobbing started to quieten. Luke calmed down.

Sebastien came closer to him and said softly. "I understand. The pain you are feeling now. It is unimaginable. You have lost the one you loved. And to make it worse, no one even knows" Luke looked up. Facing straight into the wilderness. "You do not get the understanding or the sympathy. You do not get the support. Even though your heart has been broken, you loved her even if." He paused cautiously. "She did not love you back."

After a moment, Luke whispered. "I just don't know how to make it stop. The pain. I just want to make it stop."

Sebastien sighed. "Over time, it will fade. You will move on with your life. The animal in you will adapt. It will enable you to survive. For now, though, perhaps talking about it would help?"

Considering this for a moment, Luke then nodded. Straightening himself and wiping his face. "Okay", he said weakly.

"Is there any reason you can think of why someone would want to hurt Jessica?" Sebastien asked.

"No," Luke replied strongly. "None at all. I cannot think of why anyone would want to hurt her. Everyone likes her."

"You sure there were not any rows? Any minor disagreements that happened?",

"No. She did not argue with anyone. She was too nice for that. And too fun. She would not take anything seriously enough to argue about it."

Sebastien nodded. "Is there anything else you can think of? Before or during the party? Anything that struck you as odd? That could be relevant. Even if you think it is insignificant," Sebastien pressed.

"Well, I do not think so," Luke said. He scrunched his face. Creasing his forehead and thinking deeply about the question.

"Okay, well…"

"Actually," Luke interrupted. "There may be one thing. It is probably nothing, but you said anything."

"Yes?" Replied Sebastien eagerly.

"Well, it is just at the party. When we were in the huddle just before she died, we were all talking; I can't remember what about now. Anyway, Jess said something funny. In response to that, Kate reached over and grabbed her wrist while laughing. Again, it is probably nothing at all. I guess it is just that it was the hand that she was holding her glass with. I don't know if that could be relevant."

Sebastien was deep in thought. Taking the information in. "It could be," He said quietly. "It could be very relevant." He looked back to Luke. "And can you think of any reason why someone would want to hurt Rebecca?"

"Rebecca?" Luke replied, confused. "Why does that matter?"

"Well, as she and Jessica were standing side by side. It is possible she was the intended victim."

"Oh God," Luke exclaimed. "So, someone could have been aiming for Rebecca and got Jessica instead. Oh god, why? Why did they have to get it wrong? Why did she have to die by mistake?" He screamed. Looking as if he may fall over again.

"Does that mean you would rather that Rebecca had died?" Sebastien asked. Staring straight into his eyes.

"Well," Luke said. Starting to appear flustered. "Not that. I mean, no one should have died. It is a horrible thing for anyone to be murdered, of course. I did not mean I wanted her to die. Just that Jessica was so…" He struggled to find the words. "Perfect," He said longingly. Looking into the distance.

Sebastien shrugged. "Of course," He said. With a thin smile. "Although there is the argument you had."

Luke turned back to him suddenly. "What do you mean?"

"Well, yesterday before the party. You and Rebecca argued in her room. Quite fiery if I remember correctly."

"I would not say it was fiery. I am not sure where you are getting your information from."

"I can assure you that my sources are impeccable. You and Rebecca argued. A heated, fiery, blazing argument."

"What exactly are you implying?" Replied Luke suspiciously.

"Well, you argue with a potential target of murder hours before the murder takes place. Then, now, you imply that it would be better if she were dead. You must admit that it does appear somewhat suspicious."

"Suspicious? Are you accusing me of murder? Of killing Jessica?" Luke's face was turning red. His breathing became heavier. His eyes fixed on Sebastien.

"Not accusing you, no. I am warning you. If we can see this, then so can others. If the police realize this, well, they will want to know what the argument was about," Sebastien reassured him calmly.

Luke contemplated this for a moment. As he saw Sebastien's point, he started to calm down. He started to understand the danger this put him in.

"The argument? That was nothing, really. Nothing important," He said, rather flustered. "One of those things that seems important at the time but later you release really isn't. You know what I mean?"

Sebastien nodded. "Of course. I have these moments from time to time. So what was it about?"

"What was it about?" Luke repeated. Appearing slightly confused.

"The argument. If it was not important, surely there is no harm in telling us."

Luke hesitated. His face appeared frozen for a few moments. "Yes… the argument. It was rather silly, really. I… just happened to be a bit annoyed with her, that's all. You see, Rebbeca and I did a group project together at uni. Anyway, it did not go very well. We got a lower mark, which brought down my grade for the whole module. So, I was naturally upset. I thought she had not contributed enough, and so I blamed her for our failure. But now, looking at it, it is not important. It was only one module. So, you see, it was nothing really."

After listening carefully all the way through and focusing on his words, once he finished, Sebastien paused for a moment before smiling. "Of course, now I understand. As you said, it was nothing. Thank you for putting my mind at rest."

"No problem," Luke replied, smiling nervously. "Anyway, I must get back to the house. But please do not let me stop your walk. See you later," He said. Darting off back in the direction of the house before they could stop him. Clearly keen to get away.

Looking after him. Archie said. "Well, he was clearly lying."

"Yes. You are right," Replied Sebastien. "About his argument, yes, he was certainly lying. But about his feelings for Jessica. No, he was certainly not."

"How did you know she did not love him back?" Archie asked. "I mean, I understand how you got that he loved her. But nothing to me showed that she did not love him?"

"Well, I was not certain. Not until I said so and he did not deny it. But if they did love each other. Why would they keep it a secret? They are both friends of the same age. Single, as far as we can tell. Why would they not share it with their family and friends? It just seemed most likely that the love was one-sided."

"Well, that rules him out for wanting Jessica dead."

Sebastien looked at him. "Does it?"

"Well, if he loved her, why would he want to kill her?"

"Love. It is the most powerful thing. It can make us do things that we cannot imagine. And turn us into something that we could never have predicted." He pauses. "Imagine that Luke professes his love to Jessica, and she rejects him. Humiliates him and breaks his heart. He then retreats into a cycle of self-pity, anger and bitterness. The feelings of love he once felt for her turn into hate. He then decides that as he cannot have her, no one can. He decides to kill her. Is that not possible?"

"Well, I suppose so," Archie accepts. "But all that we just saw. How distraught he was. How devastated. Could that really have been an act?"

Sebastien considers this for a moment. He then shrugs. "That I do not know. You are right, though. If that was a performance, then he is certainly a great actor."

CHAPTER 28

"You know what?" Sebastien says.

"No, try me?" Archie replies.

"I am still starving. I never did manage to eat that breakfast."

"Oh, I know. Me too. I mean, I know there has been a murder. But seriously. Can't the interrogations start after we have had our eggs?"

Coming back through the grounds towards the house. Both Sebastien and Archie hope there is still some food left in the dining room. After missing both dinner last night and breakfast today, they both feel light on their feet. What they see ahead of them, however, soon banishes the thought from Sebastien's mind.

"Look," Says Archie. Pointing in front of them.

Ahead, a slim young woman with chestnut brown hair is walking over the grass. She looks around at the landscape as she goes. Taking it all in.

"That's Kate, isn't it?" Archie asked.

Staring ahead, Sebastien nods. "Yes, that is her. Getting some fresh air, I suppose. A good thing to do rather than being stuck in the house all day."

He pauses for a second. Caught up in thought. He then turns to Archie and cocks his head to her. "Come on." He walks forward to catch her.

"Wait. What are we doing?" Archie calls behind him. "Can't we at least get some breakfast first?" before following on behind.

"Kate," Sebastien calls as they get closer. She turns round. Rather startled at being snapped out of her trance. Her mind was focused on the surroundings. Taking her away from the present. She looks slightly better than before. There is no redness or bags around her eyes today. The fact that she has not been crying and has managed to get a decent sleep suggests she is feeling a bit better and that she is starting to get over her loss. Or that she is confident that she has got away with it.

"Oh, hello," She said politely—a bit taken aback by seeing them.

"Yes, hello. It is beautiful, isn't it?" Sebastien replied. Gesturing to the landscape.

"Yes. You don't quite realize how beautiful it is until you leave. Before, you just take it for granted. It is so peaceful. So mindful. You can just let it suck all your worries, your concerns, out of you."

Sebastien considered this for a moment. "So, what is it that you are worried and concerned about?"

"Well, all this, of course." She said, gesturing around them. Clearly irritated about having been brought back to the topic she was desperately trying to avoid. "What happened last night"

"The murder last night makes us feel many things. It makes us mourn what we lost. It makes us sad about life that was cut short. It makes us angry at the person who decided they had the right to take a life too soon. But it does not make us worry or feel concerned." Sebastien paused. "Not unless there is a reason for it to do so."

Kate looked at him. Clearly suspicious. "What is it that you want?" She asked curtly.

"What I want is to know why Jessica's death makes you worried?"

"That," Kate spluttered. "That was just a turn of phrase."

"No, it wasn't," Sebastien countered. "You know it wasn't. Something is making you worried. Something so important that now the immediate shock of Jessica's death is wearing off; it is taking over, even over the death of your best friend. So, the question is, what is that important?" He turned towards her. She remained silent. He shrugged. "Someone cynical may say that perhaps it is a fear of being discovered, of being found out."

Her eyes widened. Her shock was clear on her face. "You think I did it? You think I killed her?" She screamed.

"What I think is that you are hiding something. Something that could be related to Jessica's death. Maybe something that gives you a motive for it. That is what I think!"

Kate turned away. Avoiding their eyes. "This is ridiculous.

Absolute rubbish. I am hiding nothing," She said. Appearing offended.

Sebastien sighed. "Ok, perhaps I will just go and speak to Tony."

Kate whipped around. Panic on her face. "What...Why would you do that?"

Sebastien smiled. "I just have a feeling that he could fill in some of the gaps you are leaving for me."

Kate's shoulders fell. She let out a deep sigh. "How do you know?" She asked. Her tone made her sound exhausted.

"When we spoke before you were very keen to move on from the subject of Tony. You were quick to point out that you do not know him well. Even though you have been coming here since you were a child, it suggested there is more than meets the eye."

"When I was in London," She began. "Tony came into the café where I work one day. We got talking and ended up spending the night together. I don't know how it happened, really. It just did. It was exciting, and he was so charming. This sophisticated older man. It just felt right. Anyway, we met a few times more. We had fun. And then..." She cut off.

"And then you came back to Claytons. Back to a world where your affair was not easy to hide. Where if it were found out, it would have consequences."

She nodded. "I have just been so anxious. Wondering every moment if Imogen knows. So frightened of slipping up. Of revealing something that lets it all come out. It has been nerve-racking."

Sebastien nods sympathetically. Understanding her troubles. Thinking carefully about what to say next. "Jessica?" He finally says. "Did she know?"

Kate lets out a cry. "I don't know how. Maybe she saw us together sometime in London or heard from someone. But she knew."

"She told you so?"

"No. We were walking when I arrived. It was wonderful. We were chatting and catching up. Then she started talking about forbidden love. About an affair, it feeling so right, but it is actually wrong, that it makes you guilty. That you need to tell the truth. Because you must do the right thing."

Sebastien considered all this carefully. "And you thought Jessica would tell her aunt about your affair?" He concluded.

"Well, of course. That was what she was saying. That even though me and Tony felt it was right to cheat on Imogen. It was actually wrong. She knew that, and she felt guilty about keeping the secret from her aunt. We should feel guilty as we were keeping it from her as well. That she was going to tell her aunt because it was the right thing to do."

Sebastien nodded, taking it in. "And this was something you wanted to avoid?"

"Of course it was. I have known these people all my life. They know my family. My parents. God, I never wanted them to find out. It was all just a big mistake. It was stupid. I just wanted to forget it. For it to stay in the past."

"And now Jessica threatened that," Sebastien remarked.

"I would not kill her over it." Kate protested. "Yes, I did not want it coming out. Would you? When it is so closely related to your family? Your friends? But I would not hurt her. She was my friend. My best friend. I just wanted to talk to her. To make her see sense. I hoped she would understand that it was all finished now, and telling Imogen would just cause her pain. That is what I wanted to do. But I did not get the chance." Kate looked into the distance. Remembering what she had lost.

"I believe you," Sebastien said softly. "I believe that you did not want to kill Jessica. But there is one other thing you must tell us. Something that I know you are not being truthful about."

Kate looked at him. She looked broken and desperate. Wide-eyed and brimming with tears. She nodded. "Okay. What do you want to know?"

"Rebecca. What was it that Rebbeca did to you? What made you hate her so much?"

Kate let out a small laugh. "That? Despite everything that's happened. That still fills me with rage. I know it should mean nothing after what happened to Jess. But it doesn't. She still betrayed me. Destroyed me"

Sebastien waited patiently. He let her take her time.

"When we finished college, we both applied to Oxford— law at Merton College. I was so excited. I have always dreamed of being a lawyer. Defending the innocent and fighting the guilty. I wanted to help people. To make a difference. And the law was how I wanted to do it. It was all I ever wanted. So, we both went through the admissions process. We both had top grades, aced the interviews and completed the admissions exam."

Kate's face hardened. Her voice became harsher. "I guess she must have felt threatened by me. Competition was fierce, and there were only a limited number of places. A few hours after I had completed the admissions exam, I was invited back to the college. I was so excited. I thought they were going to offer me a place. How wrong I was." She sighed. "They said that they had been tipped off by another student that I had cheated on the exam. I denied it, of course. It was ridiculous. Then, they presented the statement from Rebecca. She said she had seen me use a mobile phone in the exam to cheat. I could not believe it. She had lied. She had told them I cheated to get me disqualified from the exam. Anyway, they asked to search my bag. I let them; I had nothing to hide. They found a mobile phone in there. Different from the one I handed in. In the search history were legal texts relating to questions in the exam. I did not understand it at first. How could that have been in there? Then I remembered. Just after the exam, Rebecca watched my bag while I was going to the toilet. She must have put it in then. Once they found it, they took it as proof. I was disqualified. That was when it was over. Once that happens, no other university will touch you. My dreams of becoming a lawyer. A brilliant career. They were all gone. And why? Because she decided I was a threat to her. That I had to be stopped."

She stared at Sebastien defiantly. "There. That is the truth."

He looked deep into her eyes as if he was trying to see into her mind. As if he wished to read her thoughts. After a few moments, he nodded. "Thank you," He said. "That cannot have been easy."

She nodded in agreement before turning and walking back towards the house. After she had taken a few steps, she stopped and turned round. "There is perhaps something else you should know."

They turned to her. She has got their attention.

"When we were talking at the party. Before Jessica died, I saw Daniel with a vial of clear liquid in his hand. It only occurred to me recently. Once I had calmed down," She paused. "I am only telling you this for Jessica." After finishing this statement. She turned and continued her journey.

"God," Archie said. Once, she was out of earshot. "Uncle Tony. I would never have thought."

Sebastien put his hand on his friend's shoulder. "Unfortunately, people have an unending capacity to surprise us." He said.

"Yeah, it seems so," Archie agreed. Changing the subject, he asked. "So, do you believe her?"

Sebastien nodded. "Yes. I think her affair with your uncle and the story she told us about Rebecca were true. She seemed authentic to me."

"Yes, I agree. And so that gives her motive for both of them," Archie said.

"Yes, it does. She could have wanted to kill Jessica to hide the affair. Or she could have wanted to kill Rebecca in revenge for ruining her career."

"But would she? She seemed authentic, like you said. She said that she would not kill Jessica over the affair. Could she be lying? And with Rebecca. She gave us the story so easily. Would she have done that if she had tried to kill her?"

"Not unless she was tricking us. By making us think that she cared about keeping her affair secret less than she really did. Or she gave us the story about Rebecca more easily to make us think she could not have wanted to kill her. Perhaps it was all a ruse," Sebastien said.

"Quite," Archie agreed.

"And there is another possibility, I am afraid?"

Archie frowned.

"The affair does give your uncle motive. Is it possible that he would want to keep the affair secret enough that he would kill her?"

"Uncle Tony? No, He would not do a thing like that," Archie protested.

"I know he is your uncle. But he does have a motive. We must consider it," Sebastien said.

"But he does not have the opportunity," Archie reminded him. "He was not anywhere near Jessica when she died. And as we established earlier. It had to be one of those in that immediate group."

Sebastien nodded. "Yes, you are right. If he was involved. He could not have done it alone."

"Anyway, what about Daniel? The vial? Surely, he did it. I mean. Why else would he be carrying a glass vial at a drinks party?"

"Well, we do not know," Sebastien said thoughtfully. "We shall have to ask him to find out."

CHAPTER 29

After searching the house and grounds, Daniel was nowhere to be found. Thinking that this most likely meant he was staying in his room. Sebastien and Archie found Imogen and asked her where that was.

Walking up the stairs to his room. Archie and Sebastien chatted.

"Surely, this puts an end to it," Archie said. "He was seen with a vial of poison right before someone was poisoned. It is not hard to work out."

"Yes. You are right. That would certainly suggest that he is the culprit. But we are not yet certain whether he was carrying a vial of poison or not. At this moment, the liquid that the vial contains is unknown. So currently, we can assume nothing."

"Unknown? Come on, Seb. What else would he be carrying in a glass vial?"

Sebastien sighed. "If there were not a poisoning, then poison would be the last thing we would think would be in the vial. The only reason you think that vial contains poison is because of that event. There could be any number of innocent possibilities. A type of medicine or remedy, for example."

"Did he seem ill to you?"

"No. But not all illnesses are plain to see. Especially in someone so arrogant."

Having reached the door. They paused before they entered. They look at each other and prepare each other to go in.

Sebastien knocked on the door.

"Who is it?" Daniel called out.

Upon that invitation, Sebastien opened the door, and they went in together.

Daniel was laid on his back. On top of his duvet. Looking at his phone. "Come in then, why don't you." He said sarcastically, having seen them enter.

"Sorry to interrupt you, but there was something we needed to ask you. You had a small vial at the drinks party yesterday. What was in it?"

Daniel stared at him. Before cracking a smirk and mockingly saying. "Do you? Well, again, you must be mistaken. I did not have a vial of anything."

Sebastien's face was serious. His muscles become tense. His eyes cut into Daniel like daggers. "Then you are lying to us again." He said fiercely.

"How dare you?" Daniel spat out. "I do not have to answer to you."

"No, that is true," Sebastien agreed. "You do not have to answer to us. But you will have to answer. We may be the more favourable option."

"The favourable option? Against what? The Spanish Inquisition?"

"This is no time for jokes," Sebastien shouted. His patience had snapped. "A young woman has died. Murdered. And all you can do is make sarcastic comments. It is disgusting. And it is not in your interest. There is a convincing witness who swears they saw you with a glass vial of clear liquid at the party. It does not take a genius to put the dots together and conclude that it contained poison and you are the murderer. Trust me; your attitude will damn you."

Daniel's eyes were fixed on him. "It did not kill her," He said through gritted teeth.

"Then tells us what was in the vial!" Sebastien smashed back. His fury was clear from his face.

Daniel sighed. For the first time, his fear was showing on his face. "It was not poison in the vial. I never wanted to hurt Jessica."

"Then what was it!"

"It was LSD."

Sebastien and Archie looked at each other.

"So why did you bring that to the party?" Sebastien said calmly. His display of anger achieving what he intended.

"I wanted to drug Rebecca. There, I said it," He admitted childishly.

"Why?" Sebastien pressed.

"Because she humiliated me, alright."

Sebastien and Archie were both silent. Their stares burrowed into him.

He sighed deeply. "When we were at university. We went out. Dated. I thought it was going well. That she liked me, but it was nothing," He said bitterly. "It turns out that she actually fancied another member of the rugby team. She wanted to make him jealous. And it worked. The moment he was interested in her, she dropped me. Just like that. So there. That's why I wanted to ruin her special day."

Sebastien nodded. "You wanted her to cause a scene at her birthday party. So, you planned to put her under the influence of a drug that would cause this effect by spiking her drink. Because she rejected you?"

Daniel nodded sheepishly.

"If she has this boyfriend," Archie said skeptically. "Then why is he not here?"

Daniel smirked. "She got bored of him after a while. It seems that it did not meet her standards."

"How do we know that you are not lying?" Archie persisted. "For all we know, that vial did contain cyanide, and you are trying to trick us."

Daniel lept off his bed suddenly. He went over to his bag at the side of the room. He rifled through it furiously before pulling out a glass vial. He then strode over to Archie and held it right in his face.

"Go on. Take a look."

Rather taken a back, Archie took hold of the vial. Taking the top off. Sebastien came over and smelled the liquid. "No almonds," Sebastien muttered. Archie nodded and gave the vial back to Daniel.

"See no poison," he said desperately.

"No," Sebastien replied. His emotionless face stared into Daniel. "Just a dirty little drug being used by a sad little man."

Without another word, he left the room, and Archie followed.

"Well, we were right," Archie said once they had left. "He is a prick."

"Yes," Sebastien agreed. "It was sickening."

"Shame, really. I thought he had done it," Archie remarked.

"Well, we cannot be sure that he did not," Sebastien replied.

"What? But he showed us the vial? You said yourself that it did not smell of almonds. So, it could not have contained Cyanide."

"Well, yes. Unless it was a double bluff."

Archie looked at him, confused. Sebastien continued.

" He could have used a vial of Cyanide to poison her. But then, suspecting someone may notice him with a vial in his hand. He produces an identical replica that does not contain poison to explain away why he has the vial. A double bluff. First, he lies about having a vial at all, and then he lies, saying there was no poison in it and proving this is using the replica."

"Oh, I see. So, he did do it then?"

"I don't know. We cannot know that. All that we know is that he could have lied to us in there. He could also have told us the truth. At the moment, we just do not know."

Archie sighed. "This is all so confusing. I am struggling to keep track."

Sebastien laughed. "Don't worry, my friend. Just know that at the moment, any of them could have done it."

"Well, it is good to know we have narrowed it down," Archie replied sarcastically.

"Now, now. We will narrow it down. We just need to know more. That is all," Sebastien paused. " There is one thing that we cannot find."

Archie frowned. "What?"

"Daniels's motive for Jessica. For Rebecca, it is clear, but Jessica, no. Nothing we have seen indicates any reason why he would want to harm her."

"Maybe he doesn't. Maybe he accidentally poisoned the wrong one, like we thought. As you said, it was busy, and they could not look to see where their hands were going, and he is an idiot. I would say out of all them, he is the most likely to get it wrong."

Sebastien dwelled on this for a moment. "Perhaps," He said

thoughtfully. "It could be. But next, we must find the last piece of this particular part of the puzzle."

"What do you mean?"

"We now know why Kate was lying. We now know why Daniel was lying. But we do not yet know why Luke is lying. About Jessica, yes, he is telling the truth. But about Rebecca. No. Absolutely not. And until we know why, we will get nowhere."

"Well, at least we know who to find next."

"Yes, but first, let's get some food. Any longer, and I will collapse."

CHAPTER 30

As the breakfast had been cleared away from the dining room. Sebastien and Archie had to settle for some toast and jam from the kitchen. The thought of this, compared to the cooked food they almost had, made Sebastien almost wish he had continued his meal before. Almost. As he was still focused on what he had learned and what he now intended to find out.

Having finished their toast, they both went in search of Luke. This was not as hard as their previous search. They found him in the lounge. Curled into the same armchair, Daniel had used the night before. A glass of water was gripped in his hand. His eyes stared straight ahead.

Without asking, Sebastien sat down on the sofa in the corner closest to Luke. Archie followed suit, sitting next to him. Sebastien paused a moment. Taking in the silent man before him. He still appeared to be grieving. But now it seemed he was more peaceful. The shock has worn off. It appeared that he was now going through the motions of grief and having moved past the anger and intensive pain. He was now in the stage of sorrow. Coming to terms with what he had lost. Maybe dwelling on the good times of the past that he had shared.

Sebastien sighed. He did not like having to bring someone out of a state like this. One where they were in mourning. Grieving at the core of their being for the person they had lost. But he had some questions he needed answered. Questions that if he truly loved her, he would answer. For nothing apart from exposing her murderer could matter more.

"Luke," Sebastien said softly. "You did love her, didn't you?"

Luke turned his head. His blank, empty eyes looking at Sebastien. No recognition. He does not react to his surroundings. His thoughts completely focused on the memories in his mind until Sebastien had drawn him out.

"Love her?" Luke said weakly. Appearing slightly confused. His mind is not fully back in the present. "Yes, of course, I love her. I told you."

"Then why are you lying to us?" Sebastien asked. His eyes searched deep into Luke's. Wanting to understand his response fully.

Luke's eyes widened slightly. His attention was drawn

fully. He took a slight gulp in his throat. "Lied to you? I haven't lied to you. I told you I loved Jessica, and I did."

Sebastien cocked his head to one side. He paused for a moment, which created a feeling of dread in Luke that he was struggling to bear.

"About Jessica, you were, yes. But not about Rebecca. Why?"

Luke was silent. He was lost for words.

"If you loved her," Sebastien said softly. "If you truly loved her like I believe you did. Then why are you lying now? Why are you stopping us from finding her killer? Nothing can matter more than that. Not to you. If you loved her, then you must speak. You must tell us the truth. Why do you really hate Rebecca?"

Luke fell back into his chair and sighed deeply. "I didn't mean to lie. Really, I didn't. It was just once you made me realize that Rebecca could have been the intended victim. I panicked. I knew that if I told you the truth, it would give me a motive. It would make me even more of a suspect." He hung his head down. Ashamed of his selfishness. Feeling the guilt.

"We understand. It is natural to be scared. But you must be honest with us now. For Jessica. What had Rebecca done to you?"

Luke looked up. Desperation in his eyes. "She ruined my prospects. She tarnished my career."

Sebastien looked at him sympathetically. "Go on," He said gently. Leaning back in his seat. Ready to listen.

"Rebecca and I both study Law at Oxford." Luke began. "Naturally, we are both ambitious and want to succeed in the field. I guess I just underestimated how far she would go to make sure she would. You see, to get ahead, work experience is vital. So, we both wanted to get an internship at one of the top city law firms. It would be amazing. It would be such a great asset to have. We would learn so much. They may have even offered us a job if they were impressed at the end of it. So, we both applied. We went through the process of interviews and managed to get down to the last two. That is when we learned there was only one spot left." Luke gave a shallow laugh. "I thought she had taken it well. That she had the mentality of letting the best person win. But really, she was plotting. Scheming. She was preparing my downfall." He paused. Lost in thoughts of what had happened and his hatred because of them.

"What did she do?" Sebastien prodded gently.

Luke's gaze returned to him. "She set me up. You see, the last stage of the application process is a presentation. They give you a hypothetical legal scenario. You then have to plan and present a legal strategy to meet our client's aims. It was a test of our legal aptitude. So, I received my task. I went away and researched. I planned a strategy. Rehearsed my presentation dozens of times. Determined to get it absolutely right. I wanted this position. I needed it. I was going to let nothing stop me from giving my best. Of course, Rebecca had other ideas. You see, I arrived for my appointment. I was shown in and started my presentation. But they stopped me after a few minutes. You see, what I had prepared was not what they asked for. They had sent me a different task. I froze. I was speechless. My mouth went dry, and I lost my words. I just did not understand. How could this have happened? They sent me a letter telling me exactly what they wanted, and I had prepared exactly for that. But that was enough. You see, attention to detail is key in law. How can you trust someone to be across the details of highly complex cases if they cannot pay attention to simple instructions? No, in their eyes, I had shown a lack of consideration of the information: a lack of preparation and planning. I had appeared incompetent and inept. In that highly competitive world, it was just not good enough. I was finished."

They were silent for a moment. An uncomfortable atmosphere fills the air. It is poisoned by the reveal of this betrayal.

"I can understand why this upset you," Sebastien said. Breaking the tension. "You lost the opportunity you were so desperate for. But how does this relate to Rebecca?"

Luke lifted his head back. He closed his eyes—an expression of exhaustion appeared on his face. "At first, I did not think it did," He said before lowering his head down. "I just thought it was some mistake. That there had been some error. I called the firm. I told them this and begged them for another chance. But I was rejected. They told me there had been no mistake and the position had already been filled. Later, I found out that it had been given to Rebecca. I was around here, actually. Not at Clayton's. But near Dartmoor in the holidays. We saw each other at a social gathering. She told me about her news, and I congratulated her. I then told her about my problems, and she said that these things happen. Just after saying this, she gave me this look. This sort of sly smile. It was then that I knew. I could see it in her face and her eyes. She had done it. She had stitched me up. She swapped my letter. It made me make a complete fool of myself. So she could get it. I did not know exactly how. But I knew she did." He turned his head back to Sebastien. His eyes focused on him. "So there. That is the truth. She tricked me. It ruined my reputation when my career was most vulnerable. So, I hate her."

Sebastien met his eyes. Studying them for a moment and taking these last few words in. Finally, he nodded.

"Thank you," He said. "Now, I understand." He then sat there. Considering what he had learned.

"Of course, when it comes to reputations. It should not really be me that she is interested in," Luke remarked with a smile.

This caught Sebastien's attention. "What do you mean?" He asked.

"Her dad," Luke replied. "His firm is facing a big malpractice case. One of their clients is suing them. From what I hear, the rest are jumping the ship before it sinks." He failed to hide his satisfaction at her family's demise.

"Really. How interesting that is," Sebastien remarked. "Very interesting indeed."

CHAPTER 31

"So," Archie says excitedly as they walk away from the Lounge and Luke. "She cheated and tricked him out of his dream as well."

"Yes, it turns out that your cousin has been very busy of late. Just perhaps not in the best of ways."

Archie sighed. "It is a shame that she is such an awful person. Of course, I always knew she was selfish and ambitious. But this. I never suspected that she could be so cruel."

"Yes," Sebastien agreed absently. "It is rather sad, isn't it?"

"Which part?" Archie asked.

"Well. This was her party. Her 21st birthday. And all the friends she has here all seemed to hate her. More than that, they all have reasons to kill her. It is somewhat depressing. To see that this is all she has"

Archie considered this for a moment. "Yes, you're right," He agreed. "But it is all her fault. If she had been nicer, then she would still have her friends."

Sebastien nodded. "Yes, I guess so. It just seems such a sad way to live. Anyway, we must focus," He said strongly, turning back to the matter at hand. "We now know this. Kate had been cheated out of her chosen university course by Rebecca. Daniel had been used to making another man jealous and humiliated by Rebecca. Luke had been set up to lose his desired internship by Rebecca. All these three people have motives to kill Rebecca. But yet, she did not say this. Even once we explained why we were concerned for her safety, she rejected it. Hiding her sins was more important in her mind than any perceived threat to her life. Or even finding the murderer of her cousin. And then there is what Luke just told us. Her Father's business troubles. Financial ruin is a threat to the whole family. Does this give her a motive? Do she or her parents gain financially from Jessica's death? This is what we must find out."

Having decided on their next move. Sebastien and Archie went in search of Rebecca. Her bedroom was thought of as a good place to start and was, in fact, where it ended as well.

When they reached the door, Sebastien knocked two times. "Yes, come in." They entered to find her packing her suitcase, folding her clothes, and layering them neatly in the bag.

They were confused. "Are you going somewhere?" Sebastien asked suspiciously.

"Yes, back to Oxford," Rebecca replied casually. Not taking her eyes from her packing.

"Really. This soon. Surely you would like to stay with your family. So soon after such a tragic loss."

"Well, the police still have her body. So, we cannot even plan a funeral yet until that is released. Which I will come back for, of course. But I see no point in just hanging around here waiting for that. Mum and Dad understand. It is what Jessica would have wanted."

Sebastien thought it unlikely that Jessica would be concerned with her cousin's travel arrangements. Especially when she was still in the morgue, but he said nothing.

"Well, in that case, we hope you have a pleasant journey. But there are still one of two things we wish to ask you before you go."

Rebecca sighed. Clearly irritated by this request. "Do you really? I have answered all the questions you asked me before. I really can't think of anything more to say."

Sebastien shrugged. "Well, after some other discussions, we have some new questions that we need answered. It will only take a moment." Before she could object, he took a seat on the bed. Making it clear he was going nowhere. Archie went and leaned against the wall, his eyes fixed on his cousin. Before she could object, Sebastien began. "So, why did you lie to us?"

Rebecca turned to him. Shocked. "What do you mean? I haven't lied to you?"

Sebastien looked at her skeptically. "You said to us that there was no one with a grudge against you."

"Yes," She replied. Looking between the two of them. "So?"

"So, we know this to be a lie."

Rebecca scoffed. "I do not know what you are talking about." She said in an offended manner.

"Really, so you did not cause Kate to be disqualified from her admissions exams? Or cheat Luke out of his internship?"

She looked straight at him. The shock was clear on her face. She turned to Archie. "Surely you do not believe this rubbish?' His face did not move. His eyes glued to her.

She turned back to Sebastien. "Listen, I did not cause Kate to be disqualified. She cheated, and I merely did the right thing and exposed it. I mean, how would it be fair if I didn't? On me and everyone else who revised and worked hard to get in?"

"She claims that you framed her," Sebastien cut in.

"And as for Luke." She continued. Ignoring his interruption. "It is not my fault that he did not read his instructions properly. He made a mistake, and he wants someone to blame. So, of course, as I got it, it is going to be me. I mean, honestly. I am not responsible for their mistakes. They are adults. They are responsible for what happens in their lives. No one else."

"And Daniel?" Sebastien asked. "He claims you used him to attract another man? Leaving him without a second thought? Humiliating him?"

Rebecca scoffed. "Any woman who rejected Daniel would be humiliating him in his mind. You have met him. The man has an ego bigger than this house. I was dating him, yes. But then I met someone else I liked more. So, I broke up with Daniel. Is that wrong? Can't a young woman change her mind and decide to end a relationship? This is not 1720."

Sebastien nodded. Considering all she had said. "No," He concluded. "You are quite right. Let's move on to your father."

Her expression became confused. "My father?" She asked. "What about him?"

"Well, I heard he is having some unfortunate business difficulties. I hope he and your mother are okay?"

She paused. Her eyes flicked between her two accusers. "That?" She finally said with an uneasy smile. "Oh, that isn't anything serious. It is just a disgruntled client who lost his case. No. I appreciate your concern, but we are all fine. Well, in that way, anyway."

Sebastien continued to stare at her for a few moments as if he were staring straight into her soul. Then he suddenly smiled. "Yes, of course. Well, I am glad to hear it," He said, rising from the bed. She smiled thinly in return.

"Just one more thing?" He asked as if he had only just remembered.

"Yes," Rebbeca replied irritably.

"You and your parents. Is there any inheritance you receive from your cousin? As far as you are aware."

Rebecca frowned and shook her head. "Nope, not that I know."

"So, nothing that her parents might have left her when they died?" Sebastien persisted.

Still, Rebecca was certain. "Nope. Nothing"

Sebastien smiled. "Very well. We will leave you to your packing," He said as they both left the room.

Once Archie had shut the door behind them, he said. "So, what do you think?"

"I think she is lying," Sebastien replied. "For perhaps one of those accusations to be a lie made against her, I could maybe accept. But three. All by different people who once cared for her. No, that is not a coincidence. That is a pattern. It is repeated behaviour. No, she is still lying to us. The question is, why? These reasons create clear motives for her death, so why is she still lying to us? Is it because she is simply too arrogant, too stupid to believe someone would want to kill her? Or is it because she knows she has nothing to fear? As she knows, none of them did it. We cannot yet tell."

Archie nodded. "And about Uncle Tony? What did you think?"

Sebastien sighed. "Again, I thought she was not truthful. A moment of anxiety was clear, and her response was a little too good. It was not natural. No, there are definitely problems at your uncle's firm. Creating problems for the family. The question is whether Jessica's death would benefit the family. Could it solve their financial problems?" He turned to Archie. "Do you know if her parents were wealthy? If they had money to leave?"

Archie creased his forehead in thought. "I don't really know much about them. Only that they lived near them. Around here"

"So, they may have owned a house in Dartmoor?" Sebastien asked.

"I guess so."

"Well, if they did, then it would likely have been sold once probate was concluded. The proceeds could perhaps be put into a trust for Jessica. And Dartmoor is expensive. Being a national park. It is something to consider."

"Yes, I suppose so," Archie agreed.

"Yes, there is lots to consider. Lots indeed"

CHAPTER 32

Lying on his bed, staring at the green ceiling. Sebastien was deep in thought. The truth was that he was still as unsure of who committed the murder as he was when he started. He had discovered their motives, but there was nothing which specifically singled any of them out. And for opportunity. Well, they all had it. They all could have slipped the poison into her glass. Yes, it was extremely irritating.

A knock then came from the door. Breaking his thoughts. "Come in," he shouted out absently. Archie then bounded into the room excitedly. His energy poured out of him. "Seb, you'll never guess what's happened."

Sebastien looked up at him with an amused look. "Try me?"

"They've done it. They've found the murderer!"

Sebastien sat up suddenly. Like a spring that had uncoiled.

Sprung alert. "What has happened?" He asked Archie, turning towards him.

"Well, it turns out they got a warrant to search the whole house for the poison. So anyway, they searched Uncle Tony's and Samantha's rooms, apparently, and then they got to Luke's. They found it at the bottom of his shirt drawer. Hidden!" His face was lit up. He was clearly absorbed by the drama of it all.

Sebastien was not so joyful. He made a slight frown of concentration and nodded. "So, they have arrested him?"

"Yes, of course they have. He has been taken away."

Sebastien remained in his thoughtful mood. Considering everything he had just heard.

"You could look a bit happier," Archie remarked dryly. "They have found the murderer. It is all over."

Sebastien eyes moved. Focusing on Archie. "You think so?"

'Well, yes. They found the poison hidden in his room. They have got him bang to rights."

Sebastien frowned and cocked his head.

"Come on," said Archie. Losing his enthusiasm. He realized he was missing something. "What are you thinking?"

Sebastien hesitated for a moment. Considering what he wanted to say next. Finally, he spoke. "The poison vial? It was found in his room, in his drawers, not on him. No, I am afraid he has not been caught bang to rights. The fact is someone else could have easily entered his room and planted it there. He has been out of it for most of the day. First, as we saw on the moor and then sat in the lounge. And why would he hide it there? Surely, there are better places to hide it that would be less likely to incriminate him? He could even go out and bury it on the moor. No, I am afraid it proves nothing."

Sebastien sighed. He rose from his bed and started pacing the room. "What we do know is this. Jessica's glass could only have been poisoned once she had received it. So that means that it could only have been Rebecca, Kate, Luke or Daniel who did it. They were the only ones close enough to do so. We know Rebecca may have done it for inheritance to solve her family's financial troubles. Luke may have done it to avenge a romantic rejection. Kate may have done it to stop her secret from being exposed. And Daniel." He paused. "Well, we do not have a motive for him to kill Jessica. But that does not mean one doesn't exist. Then we get to Rebecca. Well, she could have been the intended target. We have established that the girls were close together in the circle. And that the killer would have had little sight of their hands when administering the poison. This could have resulted in a mistake. So, who would want to kill her? Luke may have wanted to kill her for tricking him out of his internship. Kate for cheating her out of her university place. Daniel, for humiliating him by casting him aside for another. As we have seen, they all harbour bitterness, resentment and anger towards her for these actions."

Sebastien stopped and grunted in frustration. "The problem is there is nothing exceptional. Nothing gives any of them more reason than the others to kill either of them. They all have opportunities. So, the thing that we must use to find the killer is motive. We must gather more information. We must find out more about the suspects. More about their relationship with the victim. And with our other potential target, for that matter."

"So how do we do that?" Archie asked.

Sebastien turned to him with a smile on his face. "Simple. We speak to the other guests at the party."

CHAPTER 33

Having decided to interview the other guests at the party. Sebastien and Archie went on their search. They did not know who they wanted to speak to first. Honestly, it didn't matter. Whatever order they spoke to them in. They would find out what they needed to know.

Walking down the corridor, they heard activity coming from the kitchen. Upon entering, they found Imogen. Her sleeves rolled up, and an apron tied around her waist, from the sight of flour, eggs, a baking tray and a rolling pin. It was safe to assume that she was baking.

"Good afternoon," Sebastien said politely as he entered. Imogen turned. She did not look well. It looked as if she had aged since the night before. Whether it was a direct effect of their ordeal or just that she could not be bothered to keep up her looks. Sebastien did not know. All he knew was that this woman had lost something that she cared deeply about.

"Good afternoon," She replied absently. Only briefly looking at him before returning her eyes to her work. "Hello, Archie," she said, having seen him.

"Oh, hello, Auntie," He replied. Slightly shocked by the scene.

"What are you baking?" Sebastien asked gently. His face showed a subtle interest.

"Just scones," She replied. Her eyes fixed on the mixture she was currently working on. "I just could not stand it. Having nothing to do. Just wallowing. Having time to think. So, I decided I would make some scones."

Sebastien nodded. "Yes, in periods like this, having time to think can be difficult. You cannot help thinking of the one thing that hurts the most."

Hearing this, Imogen tensed a little. It was clearly an experience she had felt.

"So, keeping yourself busy is probably a good idea." A small smile appeared on Sebastien's face. Imogen carried on with her work.

"It is just so shocking," Sebastien said gently. "That anyone would want to do that to such a lovely, young woman. I mean, can you think of any reason why anyone would want to hurt her?"

Imogen sighed. Her head dropped, and she leaned against the worktop. She breathed deeply. "No," she said weakly. "I cannot think of any reason why anyone would want to hurt." She paused. "None at all," She said absently.

"And there were no disagreements or arguments? Nothing at all?"

Imogen looked up at him. "No, none at all. We had not seen her in over a month. None of us had. She had been in London. How could there have been?"

Sebastien briefly considered this, then nodded. "Of course," He replied with a smile. "And her childhood friends." He continued, changing the subject. "Have you enjoyed seeing them?"

Imogen looked at him. Quite confused. "Yes," She said. Looking at him strangely. "It was nice to see them, I suppose."

"You have known them since they were young, I believe? I was told they used to visit here."

Imogen nodded. "Yes, when they were younger, they would visit to see Jessica and Rebecca. Staying in their room or going out onto the lawn." She smiled. Her head filled with happy times. "Yes, it was lovely."

"And they still got along well?" Sebastien asked.

"Yes, of course," Imogen replied defensively. "Why wouldn't they?"

"No reason. Just old friends can just have arguments from time to time. You know, the sort."

Imogen lifted herself looking superior. "I don't know what relationships you have with your old friends. But in this family, we do not argue with ours."

Sebastien paused for a moment. Thinking how wrong this was. Now they knew about Rebecca's actions. But he decided it was best not to offend her.

"Yes. I am sorry. You are probably right. My old friends

and I should have perhaps drifted apart. I am sure your family are better judges of character."

Imogen gave a satisfied nod. Pleased that her point has been accepted.

"You must have been looking forward to seeing your niece Samantha this weekend." Sebastien continued. "I am guessing it is rare, as she lives in London."

Imogen smiled. "Yes, it has been nice seeing her. Such a nice sensible young woman she has grown into. Really, that outburst after... what happened... was so out of character. She is so calm normally—a clear head in a crisis. Well, I guess something like...that...affects us all."

Sebastien nodded as she spoke. "Yes," He agreed, considering this. "Something like that affects all of us who were present." They were all silent for a moment. A dark atmosphere has come over the room. "I am glad at least that you enjoyed seeing her," Sebastien added, lightening the mood just a little.

Imogen gave a polite smile in return.

"I am afraid I must ask," Said Sebastien solemnly. "Whether you believe anyone could have any reason to harm your daughter."

Imogen's head shot up. Her body is becoming rigid and upright with anxiety. "Rebecca? What do you mean?"

Sebastien sighed. It was not pleasant having to confront the woman like this and, after the loss of her niece, having to make her aware of the threat to her daughter. But it was the only way. To find who killed Jessica and potentially prevent the murder of Rebecca. It had to be done.

"I am afraid that your niece may not have been the intended victim. She and your daughter stood closely next to each other. It is possible that the murderer intended to kill Rebecca instead."

Imogen's face turned white. A look of despair appeared on her face. "Oh god," She declared. Feeling faint, she lost her balance. Steadying herself suddenly against the worktop. Archie quickly comes to her side, supporting her.

"Please do not worry," Sebastien added suddenly. Concerned for her. "This is only one possibility merely. Why don't you take a seat?" He gestured to the table and chairs behind him.

Archie guided his aunt around the worktop and to the chair. Releasing once she was sat down. Sebastien took the seat next to her. He turned it to face her. "You must not worry," He said gently. "I understand this is easy for me to say, but it is true."

She looked at him. Staring deeply into his eyes. Desperate to know her child was not in danger. Desperate to believe that she should not worry. But still knowing that she could not.

"How can I not worry?" She asked. "Someone might want to kill my daughter. How am I not supposed to worry about that? And what can I do? She is my daughter. I am meant to protect her. Look after her. God, I could not bear the thought of anything happening to her." From her face, it was clear she meant every word. It was clear that if this happened, it would destroy her.

Sebastien put her hands on his and said gently, "It is completely natural what you are feeling. There is nothing more natural than the instinctive desire to protect your child. To be concerned by this. But there is something you can do. If you answer our questions, we can find out who did this. We can protect Rebecca."

Continuing to look into his eyes, she nodded. "You asked if anyone could wish Rebecca harm?"

"Yes" Sebastien confirmed.

"Well, I suppose I can think of two people." She said weakly. Pausing for breath.

"Take your time. We are in no rush," Sebastien reassured her.

After a few seconds, she said. "Kate might. She cheated on her admissions exam to Oxford, and Rebecca reported her. I thought she had got over it, but maybe she still resented her for ruining her plans."

Sebastien nodded. "And the other?" He pushed her carefully.

"Daniel. They were dating for a time, I believe, at university. But she decided to leave him and go for someone else. Again, I thought he had got over it. He is a handsome young man. Surely, he would have found someone else to go out with. But maybe he was still angry with her. He was always arrogant. Even when he was young."

Sebastien nodded and smiled. "Thank you," he said gratefully.

"If they wanted to kill her. Kill Rebecca. That would be

unforgivable," Imogen said—a passion coming into her voice. A fire came into her eyes. "I mean, she did nothing wrong. Kate decides to cheat, and Rebecca finds out. What was she meant to do? Just let her get away with it? No, we raised her to be fair. To do the right thing. Which is what she did. And Daniel? How dare he? My daughter does not have to settle for him. Be bound to him like a ball and chain. She is a strong, independent, ambitious woman. She is completely within her rights to change her mind. To decide she prefers someone else. What gives him the right to demand anything of her?"

Looking at her now. Sebastien saw a mother who cared passionately for her daughter. Who would back her and defend her against anyone. Even if it meant she was blind to the truth of her sins.

"Yes," Sebastien agreed. "Murder is unforgivable." He paused. "May I ask? Did Jessica inherit anything from her parents when they died?"

Imogen's rage faded and was replaced by a look of confusion. "Pardon?"

"I just wondered if she was left anything of value. Money or property, for example. I was just curious."

Imogen's eyes narrowed. "Curious why?"

Sebastien shrugged. "Well, if she had a wealth of her own, then this could create a motive?" He replies casually.

"A motive? Who? For me?" Imogen replied. Sounding offended.

"Well, that depends on whether you would stand to inherit. Would you?"

Imogen looked at him coldly. "As her next of kin, I

suppose I would inherit. But I certainly would not kill her for any amount of money."

"And did she have an amount of money?" Sebastien pressed.

Imogen sighed. "Yes. When her parents died, their house was sold. The proceeds of this were kept in trust. To be given to Jessica on her 21st birthday."

"So, she would have received her inheritance next year?" Sebastien asked.

"Yes" Imogen replied.

He nodded. "And just indulge me. As she has now died, who inherits the contents of this trust?"

Imogen looked at him with disgust. "I believe it will be split three ways. A third to myself, A third to Rebecca and a third to Samantha."

Sebastien smiled. "Thank you. You have been most helpful. We won't take up any more of your time." He then rose and immediately left the room.

Imogen looked at Archie in a disapproving manner. He smiled awkwardly and then quickly went out the door. Following his friend.

Once he had caught up, he said. "Well, I may not need to ask you to come next time. I have a feeling I might not be invited again."

Deep in thought, Sebastien missed this. "So," He said regardless. "Now we know Rebecca was lying. She does stand to gain from Jessica's death. As does her family. The question is, would she kill for it? Even with her parent's financial problems, is that enough to make her a murderer?"

"Well…" Archie began to cut in.

"And there is another point which must be considered." Said Sebastien. Too focused to hear his friend. "Were her parents involved? Just her mother? Or just her father? Or both. Did they both decide that they needed the money, and so Jessica had to die? Perhaps your uncle saw an opportunity? Two birds, one stone? Stop his affair from being revealed and solve his money troubles? All in one go." He turned to Archie, waiting for his input.

"It is possible," Archie agreed. "They could be working together. And as you said, it would solve both of Uncle Tony's problems. But if Aunt Imogen was in on it. Then, everything she did last night and how she was acting just now. It would have to be an act. I don't know. It seemed genuine to me."

Sebastien considered this. He nodded. "You are right. She may be lying. But her reaction does appear genuine. No. We have found out more, but we still do not know what the truth is. No, not yet."

CHAPTER 34

"Sorry about this. I will just finish up. Give me one moment," Samantha said.

"Don't rush. We are in no hurry," Sebastien replied easily.

Having left Imogen in the kitchen, Sebastien and Archie decided that Samantha should be the next guest they should talk to. Having found her in her room, she was just checking her medical bag. Asking them to sit as she completed her task.

"Funny," She spoke. She had a confused look on her face. "I could swear I packed five syringes, not four. Oh well, I seem to be getting everything in a muddle these days." She closed the bag and turned to them, smiling. "Sorry about that. I like to check it every once in a while to see if I need to replace anything. I guess it is the nurse in me. I always have my bag with me when we go away."

Sebastien smiled in return. "Of course. It is a rather good idea. Best to be prepared."

Samantha smiled at the compliment. "Yes, that is how I see it."

Sebastien smiled again before turning to a more serious expression. "I am afraid I would like to ask you some questions which may be unpleasant. About Jessica's death. Would you be willing to answer them?"

Samantha's face creased at the mention of Jessica's death. The event is still raw. "Of course," She said with a small nod. "Anything to help."

Sebastien nodded. "Can you think of any reason why someone would want to kill her?" Sebastien asked.

"No!" Samantha said instinctively. "None at all!"

"You are sure," Sebastien continued. "There is nothing that you can think of? Regarding her family? Or her friends?"

Samatha shook her head. "No, nothing. Jessica was such a sweet, kind girl. I can't think of any reason why anyone would want to kill her. I mean, I did not really know her friends. I have never met most of them before. And I must admit that I am not that close to my family. I guess I should be, really. But before this weekend, we had not spoken in months. Even so, I can't see why any of them would want to hurt her."

Sebastien hesitated a moment before making a small smile. "I must say. This does seem rather a change of heart."

Samantha looked at him innocently. "What do you mean?"

He shrugged. "On the night of the murder. You accuse all of her friends of poisoning her. Demanding to know which it was. Now, you say you cannot think of a motive for any of them. It just seems quite a sudden change."

Samantha blushed. "Yes, that. I must admit I did get into a

bit of a state. I mean, I had just seen Jessica die in front of me. My beautiful cousin. Dead. I guess I was just looking for someone to blame, really."

"But you were right," Sebastien stated. "Someone did poison her. And it could only have been one of those closest to her. In that group. Are you sure you didn't notice anything strange at the party? Anything at all?"

Samantha stared at him. "No. I didn't notice anything. It was all normal. It was just a nice, fun party. You saw. You were there. Before it…happened." She paused. "Anyway, I did not know any of those people. Not really. I don't know if any of them had any reason to kill Jessica. I only knew what I could see. That she was poisoned, that only they could have done it."

"Them and one other," Sebastien added.

Samantha stared at him. Unsure as to what he meant.

"Your cousin Rebecca. She was also in the group. She had just as much opportunity as the rest of them."

Samantha's face turned to shock. "You can't suspect her. Surely. She is family."

"Family members can kill each other," Sebastien said dryly. "It has been known to happen."

"Not in ours," Samantha said with offence. "We are a normal family."

Sebastien shrugged. "They usually are."

Samantha tensed. She turned away from him. Wanting to avert her eyes.

"But," He said. Deciding it was best not to offend her. He still had more to ask. "This is unlikely, as you say. For one family member to kill another. It would need something considerable. Something that we have not found," He lied.

Slightly eased by this, she turned back towards him. Still tense. Eyeing him with suspicion.

"I am afraid I must ask. Can you think of any reason why someone would wish to kill your other cousin, Rebecca?"

Becoming confused, Samantha asked. "Rebecca? Why do you want to know?"

"I am afraid she could have been the intended victim. She and Jessica were standing next to each other. It is possible that they got the wrong glass."

"Oh god," Said Samantha. Staring into space as she took this in. "How awful!"

"Quite," Sebastien agreed. "So, can you think of any reason?"

She returned to him. "No. I mean, I can't think of any reason why anyone would want to hurt her. I don't know her that well. As I said, I don't really know any of them very well. But I can't see why anyone would want to kill her."

Sebastien nodded. "You know, I am just curious." He said with mild interest. "Are you aware of the inheritance of Jessica's estate?"

She stared at him. Suspicious of where he was going with this. "No. Why would I?"

"Well. It is just that you inherit a third of her estate."

"Oh. Well, I did not know that. Anyway, I can't see how it would matter. She was a twenty-year-old. She has nothing of value."

"Oh, on the contrary," Sebastien corrected her. "She has the proceeds of the sale of her parent's property. A substantial amount, I believe. Of which you now get a share."

Her eyes pierced him like daggers. Her face tenses greatly. Becoming red. "What exactly are you implying?" She demanded angrily.

"Nothing," Replied Sebastien innocently. "I am merely stating a fact. That now your cousin is dead. You stand to inherit a share of her trust. I was merely curious as to if you knew."

"You mean you were merely curious as to if I had a motive for her murder," Samantha said harshly.

"Well, I suppose so, yes. As you have said, it does give you a motive."

Her face became increasingly dark. "So that is what you think? That I would kill my cousin for money? You are sick."

"No," Sebastien replied. "I just…"

"It is disgusting. We are here grieving, having lost a beautiful member of our family. Far too soon. And what do you do? Accuse us. Interrogate us. It is revolting."

"Please," Sebastien cut in. "I did not mean to offend you. I just…"

"And how could I have even done it?" Samantha continued in a rage. "You said yourself. Only one of those close to her could have done it. I was talking to you both, for god's sake. Have you ever thought of that?"

"Well?"

"Get out!" She screamed. "Just Get Out"

They both left quickly. Fearful of what else they may encounter if they hesitated for even a second.

"Wow," Archie said. "I have never seen her like that before. It was like she was possessed."

"Yes," Sebastien agreed. Going over the conversation in his mind. "She was certainly out of character. As your aunt said,"

"It is a shame that we didn't learn anything," Archie added.

"It is right that we heard what we already knew—no new motives. There are no new disagreements. The same four suspects." He paused and sighed. "Yes, we learned very little. Just one thing."

"Which is?" Archie asked.

"She claims that she did not know she would inherit from Jessica. That is what we learned."

"Claims?"

"Yes, we cannot be certain she is telling the truth. Her display of outrage there is very convincing. But it could be an act. For someone usually so calm and collected, it does appear to be rather a different reaction than you would expect."

"She has just lost her cousin."

"Even so. For an experienced nurse. No stranger to a medical emergency. As her response at the time showed. No, it still doesn't sit right with me."

Archie shrugged. "Fine. But I still think seeing what happened could shake anyone up. And you have forgotten something."

"It may have just been the sight of the death which caused her change in behaviour." Sebastien agreed. "I just don't think it is. And what have I forgotten?"

"The four suspects? As she said. Only those close to Jessica could have done it. She was across the room talking to us when it happened."

"Yes, you are right. If it was her, then she must have had an accomplice in that group. The question is, who could it have been?"

CHAPTER 35

Some minutes later, they were walking down the corridor. When they saw Richard striding purposely towards them, his face was red, and his eyes were fixed on them. His arms swinging. Cutting the air as he walked. His body tensed like a coiled spring. His face held an expression of pure fury. All are creating an image of a man who wanted a fight.

"Now look here!" He shouted as he came within a few metres of them. "How dare you harass my wife like that. Asking her all those questions. Suggesting she could possibly be involved in this. She is now distraught. Absolutely drained. I mean, how could you? Can't you see how this whole damn business has affected her? Why couldn't you just leave her alone?"

His breathing was ragged. His eyes were still firmly fixed on them. His fury was clear from his eyes.

"Richard," Said Sebastien carefully. "I did not suggest she was involved in this. I just asked a few questions. Questions, it must be said, that will be considered by the police. I am sorry to have distressed your wife. Really, I am. But I promise you that it was never my intention."

Richard relaxed just a little. The tension in his body eased slightly, but not much. His breathing slowed as he began to calm down. "Just stay away from her!" He spat out. "Leave her alone!"

He turned to walk back just as Sebastien said. "Of course. However, there are still some things I would like to ask. Perhaps I could ask you? Then we do not need to trouble her."

Richard turned back. He looked at him in a disbelieving way. Thinking the man had a nerve. "Fine. If it means you won't bother Sam. Ask me what you like."

"Thank you," Sebastien said gratefully. "So, can you think of any reason why someone would want to kill Jessica?"

"No," Richard said immediately.

"Really? Are you sure? Nothing at all?"

"No," Richard confirmed.

"That was a very quick response," Sebastien commented. "Almost as if you did not even think."

Richard shot him a hard stare. "I did not know the girl," He growled. "I only ever met her at these bloody family things of Sams. We hardly ever see any of them. So, no. I did not need to think. I did not know any reason why someone would kill her."

"So, neither you nor your wife ever saw Jessica in London when she was studying?"

"No. London is a very big city. And we are very busy. To be honest, I did not even know she was studying there."

Sebastien shrugged. "Very well. What about your wife's other cousin, Rebecca? Can you think of any reason why someone would want to kill her?"

"Rebecca?" He said, confused. "No"

Just as Sebastien was about to speak, he added. "And no. Again, I did not need to think. Like her cousin, we barely saw her. Only at family events. Which are rare."

Sebastien smiled. "Thank you for clearing that up." He paused. "Was there anything at the party that you saw that you thought was suspicious?"

Richard sighed. "No," He said with an air of boredom. "I saw nothing unusual. Everything seemed to be normal for a party."

Sebastien nodded. "I must ask. Were you aware of how your wife benefits from her cousin's death?"

Richard's face turned to a crooked smile. "Yes, I was wondering when you would bring that up." He sneered. "No, is the answer. She did not even know herself. So how possibly could I?"

"Oh, people can find out various things about their spouses. Sometimes quite unexpectedly. It is always good to check," Sebastien says as if he was just curious.

"Well," Richard said. "If that is all?" He started turning his body away from them, clearly indicating his desire to leave.

"Yes. Of course," Sebastien replied. "Thank you for your help."

Quickly, Richard turned and walked back the way he had

come. Once he was out of earshot, Archie said. "Well, he was cheery."

Sebastien laughed, turning to him. "Yes, He was certainly angry about how we had upset his wife. It is only natural, I suppose. A husband protective of his wife's feelings."

"Us?" Archie asked. "If I remember correctly, it was you who asked all the questions. I was just tagging along. It was you who upset her."

Sebastien looked at him dismissively. "It does not matter who upset who…"

"It was you, for the record," Archie repeated.

"What is important?" Sebastien continued. "Is what we learned."

"And what did we learn?" Archie asked.

Sebastien sighed. "Not much, really. Like his wife, he knew no reasons why someone would kill Jessica or Rebecca. Again, like his wife, he did not know she would benefit. Whether that is true, we cannot say." He paused. Thinking. "There is still one key point in their defence, though. Neither of them could have poisoned Jessica's glass if either or both of them were involved in the murder. They must have had an accomplice."

"But who could that be?" Archie asked, "Perhaps Rebecca? They find out about their claim to Jessica's inheritance. They tell Rebecca. They plan the murder together. Rebecca administers the poison?"

Sebastien considered this for a few moments. "I am not sure," He said finally. "If they wanted to kill Jessica, why tell Rebecca? She would get her inheritance. Whether she knew or not. And if she were against the plan, then it would all be ruined. And why would she administer the poison on their behalf? Making herself a suspect to protect them. No. From what we have learnt about Rebecca. This does not fit. She is selfish. She would not risk herself for them. No, it just doesn't fit."

Archie sighed. "Well, what about one of the others? Maybe they administered the poison in exchange for a share of Samantha's inheritance."

Sebastien nodded. "Yes, that is more likely. It is possible that, somehow, a deal could have been struck. But again, the question is who?"

"So, what do we do now?" Archie asked.

"Now" Sebastien said. "We talk to the last guest"

CHAPTER 36

Having now interviewed all the rest. They had now reached the final guest at the party. Well, we say guest. Really, he was a co-host.

They found Tony in his study. It was one of the few rooms of the house they had not come across before in their investigations. With hard oak panelling. Shelves lined with legal volumes. And a large mahogany desk. It looked more like the office of a university professor than a city lawyer. But this was not his real office. That was in London. This was where he would come on the rare occasion that he had work to do once he had returned to Dartmoor. Perhaps it reflected more of his tastes than the image he had to maintain for his work. All the same, it was impressive.

When they had come in, Tony had welcomed them cheerily. He was at his desk on his laptop. Clearly, he wasn't the sort to take full compassionate leave. When we asked if we could ask him a few questions, he readily agreed—directing us to a pair of armchairs by the fire. He indicated to us to grab another chair from his desk so he could sit.

"So," Tony begins. "What is this all about?" He asks with a smile, always in a happy mood. But then, a successful lawyer of his experience. I think he could always portray the exact image he wanted.

"We just wondered if we could ask you a few questions?" Sebastien said. "About Jessica? Such as if can you think of any reason why someone would want to kill her?"

Now Tony's face lost its smile. Turning to a weary frown. "Oh yes," He replied. "That. It's such an awful business. But no. I cannot think of any reason why anyone would want to kill Jessica. None at all."

Sebastien nodded. "And for your daughter? I am sorry, I must ask. You see. Unfortunately, she could have been the intended victim."

His face turned to shock. Quickly being replaced by a look of concern. "Rebecca. You are sure she was the intended target?"

"No" Replied Sebastien. "But they were standing side by side at the party. Their drinks close together. It is possible the murderer selected the wrong glass."

Tony sighed. "Dear god. I did not think this weekend could get any worse." He put his head in his hands.

"Please," Sebastien said softly. "Do not be alarmed. This is only one possibility. But it is one we must consider. If you want to protect your daughter. The best thing you can do is answer our questions."

Tony lifted his head and nodded. Blinking his eyes. "Any reason someone would want to kill Rebecca?" He checked. Sebastien nodded. Tony sighed. "Listen," He continued. "I know my daughter. I love her. But it must be said she can be selfish. The fact is that she has ruthless ambition. I can see that in her. It is not uncommon in my line of work. To be honest, she probably gets it from me. But even so, I can't think of any reason why anyone would want to kill her. I mean, yes, there was that whole exam thing with Kate, and she dumped Daniel. But would they kill her over it? I just can't see it. But then again. How can I think of anyone wanting to kill my little girl?"

Sebastien nodded. Taking this in. "Yes. In my experience. People can rarely bring themselves to consider the worst-case scenario regarding those they love." He paused. "Going further. Was there anything at all at the party you noticed that was unusual?"

"Unusual? No. Everything was going as it should. People were eating and drinking and chatting and laughing. It was all going great. Until the murder."

Sebastien nodded. He took a deep breath. "I am afraid you have lied to us?" Sebastien said with certainty. Staring straight at Tony.

Tony stared straight back. Looking as if he would like to tear him to shreds. "I am not sure what you are talking about." He said in a calm tone, with just an edge of menace. "I think you must be mistaken."

"Oh, I think not. You said that you could not think of any

reason why someone would kill Jessica. But there is someone with a reason that you would have certainly known. You"

"Me?" Said Tony in surprise. A smile on his face. "What possible reason could have to hurt Jessica?"

"Well, your affair with Kate, of course."

The smile disappeared and was replaced with a frown. "That bloody girl. Why couldn't she just keep her mouth shut?"

"So, you admit it then?"

"Well, how can I not?" He shouted. "She clearly told you. How else could you know?"

"And you see what this means? Kate believes that Jessica knows about your affair and is going to tell your wife. You and Kate decide that you cannot allow this to happen. So you decide to murder her."

"No!" Tony shouted defiantly. "We did not kill her. Well, at least I didn't."

"So, you think that Kate may have done?" Sebastien asked.

Tony hesitated. "Oh, I don't know," He said desperately. "I just told her to talk to her. To deal with it. It would be more likely to work coming from her. And then Jessica is dead. Well, I did wonder."

Sebastien nods. "Well, now you have nothing to worry about. Jessica is dead, and your secret is safe."

Tony stared at him. Daring him to challenge him. "I did not kill her. Her death had nothing to do with me."

Sebastien raised his eyebrows and nodded. "And what about the other motive you have?"

"Other motive?" Tony replied with the same surprise. "I don't know what you mean?"

"I mean your business troubles. The malpractice case at your firm and the further loss of your clients following this"

Tony looked at him for a moment. His face is emotionless. His mind is calculating. Then his face relaxed and went into an easy smile. "I am still not sure what you are talking about. My firm is just fine. Over the past thirty years, I have been building it. I think you must be mistaken," He said. Finishing with a chuckle.

Sebastien remained unchanged. "Again, I think not. Although, you appear much more comfortable presenting this lie than the last. That is still what it is—a lie. Your firm is in trouble. You know that gives you a motive."

Again, Tony laughed. He looked to Archie. "Honestly, I don't know where your friend gets these ideas from." Before turning back to Sebastien. "Listen, my firm is in good health. We have a great reputation and an excellent client list. Remember the new sports centre in Exeter we talked about yesterday. It was my firm that managed the legal affairs. I was even invited to the grand opening six months ago. So, you see. My firm is doing well, and as you can see, so am I." He gestured around him generally to the house. "Honestly, there is no need to be concerned," He said in a slightly patronizing tone.

"I can assure you, I am not concerned. I am frustrated by your lies. Your firm was doing well, and so were you until this case of malpractice and the consequences that followed. But maybe you found one last hope. A source of funds, for example."

Tony stared at him fiercely.

"I am sure you are aware of the trust created after the death of Jessica's parents with the proceeds of their estate." Sebastien continued. "On the contrary, considering your legal experience, you may even manage it. And if so, then you would certainly be aware of the inheritance of this trust should Jessica die before her 21st birthday—a third for Samantha, a third for Rebecca and a third for your wife. Perhaps two-thirds of this fortune would be worth killing for at this desperate time?"

Tony's stare had remained unchanged. Only now did his face grow tenser. "You think I would kill my niece," he said in a harsh tone.

"I think desperate situations make people do desperate things."

"If the firm did go under. The inheritance from Jessica could not cover our lifestyle. So, you see, why would I kill her for it?"

"Even if it could not cover your entire lifestyle. It could, perhaps, maintain the most important part of it," Sebastien suggested. "Your home. It could allow you to keep it, even if you lost your income. So yes, I am afraid it does give you a motive."

"And how was I meant to do this? I was on the other side of the room when she died."

"Using your daughter, of course. She was with the group, and she would benefit as well. You would have been working together."

"This is nonsense. Absolute rubbish," Tony spat out.

"So, you deny it?" Sebastien said calmly.

"Yes. Of course, I bloody do," Tony hit back. "I think that is enough questions. I have work to do. Please leave"

Sebastien nodded. "Of course. I appreciate your help." He paused. "And the best of luck with it all."

Tony had already opened his laptop. Starting to work. But he lifted his eyes briefly after that last comment before returning to the grind.

Once they had left, Archie said. "Did you really have to be so hard? He is my uncle, you know. He has always supported me."

"So that means he couldn't be involved?"

"Of course not. Just that you could have been a bit kinder."

"I was kind until he started lying to me. Then what am I meant to do? Not confront him. No, I am sorry, but it had to be done. And at least we learnt something."

"What? As far as I could see, it just confirmed what we already knew."

" Yes, but there was something I heard there. I am not sure what it was, but I know it was important. It is annoying me. I am not..." Sebastien stopped. He was lost for words. "That is it... Yes, that explains it...But if that is what happened...we have been looking at this all wrong...but then how else could we look at it?" Silent again. Sebastien's mind was working fast and totally absorbing his attention.

"Seb," Archie said nervously. "What's going on?"

"What is going on is that I know!"

"You know who killed her?"

"Yes, and I know why. But I must first make a call. If the answer is what I think, it will be the proof that I am right." He turned to Archie. "Could you assemble everyone in an hour, please? Where it happened. Get them all to be there."

"Ok. But aren't you going to tell me what this is all about?"

"You will soon know. As will everyone else."

CHAPTER 37

So, back here we are again. Back in the room where the party was held. The room where Jessica was brutally murdered.

Archie was not sure why Sebastien wanted to do it here. To tell all that he knew. Surely, he could do it anywhere. The lounge would have been the natural choice. But Sebastien had insisted. He said it was important it was done here. Where she had died, Archie could not see why, but he didn't argue.

They had brought in the chairs and positioned them around the room. Forming a circle around the centre. Just as Sebastien had wanted, now, the room was full of everyone who was at the party. Getting them all to come was not easy. But in the end, it turned out to be simple. You just reminded them that it would look disrespectful, even suspicious, not to come. Once you did that, any hesitations were lost.

Now, they all sat in the circle they had arranged—an odd atmosphere in the air. There was tension because of why they were here and where they were. However, a feeling of nervousness was also shared. Nerves at what was to come next. What they would find out.

Everyone was present. The lights dim as they were at the party. The stage was set. Now, it began.

Standing in the centre of the circle, Sebastien looked around the room. Taking in the sight. All those involved in this case sat before him.

"Thank you for coming today," He began. "Back to the place where this all started." He turned. Gesturing towards the floor where Jessica had been. "Where Jessica was murdered."

A gentle sob could be heard coming from Imogen. Who was swiftly take in a hug by her husband.

"Yesterday evening," Sebastien said. Raising his head, looking back at them and turning around to move his gaze across them all. "At the party, we were all attending. To celebrate Rebecca's 21st birthday. Jessica was a happy, fun girl. Chatting with her friends, having fun, and enjoying the party. But then she takes a drink. A drink later found with traces of cyanide. After this, she then starts fitting and dies."

Sebastien pauses. Continuing to gaze around the room. "An awful tragedy to happen. A terrible crime to commit. But from this, we know a few things for certain. Firstly, that her drink could not have been poisoned before she had received it. As I saw myself, the unfortunate waiter nearly spilled his tray because he did not know she was taking a glass. No one, not the staff or any of the other guests, could have known she would take a glass. And not that specific glass. So no, to target her, they must have poisoned her glass once she had taken it. And this tells us something else."

He pointed towards the area of the room where Jessica had been standing at the party. Moving towards it. "Jesicca was stood here when she drank from the glass—in a circle, chatting. Now, if her glass was poisoned after she had received it, that means it must have been someone close to her who had done so. Someone in the circle" Everyone looked at each other. Those outside of the circle looked accusingly at those who were in it. "Yes. Only Kate, Luke, Daniel and Rebecca had the opportunity to poison Jessica's glass. Myself, Archie and Samantha were in the corner to the right," He said, pointing towards the left as he was facing the door. "Whereas Tony, Imogen and Richard were all gathered in the corner to the left." Using his other hand, he gestured in the other direction. "So that means that none of us had the opportunity to poison the glass. So, none of us could have done it. It must have been one of the members of that immediate group."

All eyes moved to these four—the tension mounting. "One of them could have easily poisoned the glass. Amongst the chatter. The laughter. The focus of the rest of the group would have been taken. They would all be distracted and stood in a circle. Their glasses were held out in front of them. In the centre. All they needed to do was slip the poison into her glass." He paused. "But it is not quite as simple as that.

Our murderer had to be clever. They had to appear completely natural. They had to be focused and engaged in the conversation. Otherwise, they would draw suspicion. Suspicion which would incriminate them once the murder had occurred. So, they had to keep their eyes fixed on the guests around them. On who was talking. Not on what their hands were doing. And this creates the potential for a mistake. You see, Rebecca and Jessica were standing next to each other. Huddled in the circle. Their glasses are close together. It is possible that the murderer chose the wrong glass. And got the wrong victim."

All eyes moved to Rebecca. Looking uncomfortable in her seat. "Yes," Sebastien continued. "This means we must now consider the possibility that Jessica was not the intended target. That Rebecca was. And so that means we must consider the motives that the others had for her murder. As well." Sebastien paused. "So, who had a motive? Who could have wanted to kill Jessica? Or Rebecca?"

He turned slowly. "Perhaps you, Kate?" He said. Resting on her. "Your motive for Rebecca was clear. She framed you for cheating at Oxford and destroyed your dreams of a legal career before it had even begun. A betrayal by someone that you trusted so closely. Which still creates such bitterness in you. Perhaps you snapped? Decided that what she had done meant she deserved to die?" Kate was emotionless. A silent defiance rose from her. "And for Jessica. Well, it was her knowledge that gave you motive."

Kate's lip started to tremble. Knowing what must come next. Tony's body grew increasingly tense. His face became red. "You believed that she knew of your affair with her uncle." Kate's face collapsed in a sigh of despair.

"Lies," Shouted Tony. His tone is venomous. Turning to his wife. Who was staring at him in disbelief. Unsure what to think. He said. "Darling, this is non-"

"Quiet," Sebastien shouted back. A hard expression on his face. An even harder edge to his voice. "There is nowhere to hide. Not now. The truth must come out—all of it. A murder changes everything." His eyes shifted to Imogen briefly. The sight of the shocked and grieving woman caused Sebastien to give a look of sympathy.

"No," Sebastien continued. Returning to the matter at hand. "You believed Jessica knew about your affair. More than that, you believed she would expose you that she would reveal your mistake. Humiliating you in front of your family. A situation you found unbearable. So, did you decide to stop that? That it was worth killing for?"

"No!" Kate shouted. Her composure had shattered. "I would never hurt Jessica. Never"

Sebastien turned again. "Or perhaps it was you, Luke." He suggested. Resting on the nervous young man. "You admit to loving Jessica and having passionate feelings for her. An intense longing to be with her. One that has caused you such pain since her death. But you also admit that she did not love you back. She did not return your affection. Rejecting you. Was this too much? Had you had enough? Did you decide that if you could not have her, no one would?"

"No!" The boy screamed in desperation. "I loved her. I still love her. It is torture being without her. I...I just wish she was still her," He whined. Breaking into a sob.

"And Rebecca?" Continued Sebastien calmly. "For her, your feelings are less friendly. She tricked you. Cheated you out of a prestigious internship. Damaging your professional reputation. Limiting your prospects. For someone as ambitious and driven as you. This deliberate sabotage. By someone you trusted. It was unforgivable. Did you decide that a lack of forgiveness was not enough? That she deserved to suffer what she had done? That she deserved to die?" With Luke still sobbing, Sebastien moved on.

"Or maybe it was Daniel who decided she had to die?" Sebastien said as he turned towards him. "Rebecca strung you along. Made you believe that she loved you. That she wanted to be with you. When all along, she was using you to get another. To make someone jealous. That is all you were needed for. And then she threw you away. For someone with your arrogance, your ego. That must have been humiliating. You must have felt raw hatred towards her. A simmering anger. Did it get too much? Did you decide that Rebecca had to die?"

Sebastien and Daniel were locked in a stare. Daniel's face was tense. His eyes are wide. Trying his best to appear unfazed. It was clear that he was furious, as if it took every ounce of his restraint not to hurl himself at his accuser.

After a few moments, caught in the stare. Sebastien shrugged and turned. "Or maybe the motive was more financial? Was it Rebecca?" He asked. Fixing her in his sights. "Your father's business troubles are causing a threat to your family's security. To your home. Did you decide that something had to be done? Did you? Someone so ruthless and calculating. Decide that your cousin's life was a price worth paying for the inheritance it would bring?"

"Stop it!" Imogen screamed. "Just stop it. How dare you

come here to our house. When we are in mourning, and accuse us. Our daughter. Of murdering her cousin. It is despicable."

Sebastien turned sharply towards his attacker. "I am afraid it is nothing of the sort." He said with certainty. "It is unpleasant, yes. But then, so is this whole affair. No, I am sorry, but your daughter had a motive. Same as all the rest of them. As I am afraid, do you?"

She stared at him in shock. "Yes," He continued. "You have the same motive as your daughter. You are terrified of how your husband's business troubles may affect your family. Whether it may mean that you have to sell your house," He said, gesturing vaguely around him. "The home that you so adore. So, did you make a choice? You knew about your niece's trust fund after her parent's death. You would have known what you and your daughter would inherit. Perhaps you decided that this was what you needed to do to save your family. Your position? Your home?"

"Absolute rubbish," Tony spat out. Putting a supportive arm on his wife. Which she readily shrugged off.

Sebastien switched his gaze. "Of course, this all applies to you as well. Your business is in trouble. Your future is uncertain. You would have also known about Jessica's trust fund and your wife's inheritance. Maybe you persuaded your daughter to slip the poison into Jessica's glass? Or maybe you used your lover? Again, you have the same motive as her. Your affair being exposed would ruin your marriage. What was meant to be a harmless bit of fun would destroy everything you cared about. So maybe you persuaded her to administer the poison? Two birds, one stone.

Although, it is not fair to say that you were the only part

of your family who benefited from Jessica's death." Sebastien turned to Samantha. "I am afraid that you, Samantha, also gained. You would inherit a third of Jessica's trust. This gives both you and your husband a motive. Perhaps you made a deal? You offered one of them. A member of the circle. A share. In exchange for administering the poison. You would pay them a reward from your inheritance."

Samantha started breathing heavily. It is becoming more rapid. Her face was turning bright red. Her eyes welled up. Her reaction to this accusation is deeply emotional. Richard brought her towards him tightly. "Don't worry. Just breathe." He turned his head towards Sebastien. "Now look what you have done," He growled. "Why can't you just leave her alone?"

Sebastien came towards her and crouched down. Taking her hand in his and looking into her eyes. "There is no need to be afraid." He said gently. "I do not think you did this. In fact, I know it. But, I do know who did."

CHAPTER 38

"Throughout this whole investigation, there were two questions that kept nagging away at me," Sebastien said, having returned to the centre of the room.

"The first is why Cyanide?" He looked around at them all. "You see, Cyanide is a fast-acting poison. It acts within seconds to minutes of when it is consumed. So why use this particular type of poison? For this murder? By using Cyanide, they narrowed down the window in which Jessica could have consumed the poison. We know that she must have consumed it in the few minutes before her death. So as her drink is the only thing she consumes; we know this was poisoned. And because only four suspects had the opportunity to poison her drink once she had it. It has narrowed down our list of suspects as well. Why? Why have they done this? With another type of poison. Perhaps a slower-acting one. They could have increased the window in which it could have been taken. They could have expanded the pool of suspects. They could have thrown suspicion off of themselves. Why have they not done this?

The second question is, why was she poisoned at the party? You see, to poison someone, you do not actually have to be there at the time. The poison can be planted, and you can leave it there. You can be a million miles away when they consume the poison and die. So why did the murderer decide to poison Jessica at the party? Again, by doing so, they narrowed down the list of suspects. They made themselves easier to identify. Suppose they had just left it somewhere for Jessica to consume another time. They could have thrown suspicion off themselves. Again, why have they not done this?"

Everyone looked around at one another. Seeing his points and seeing that they were all equally confused. "The answer is," Sebastien continued. "That it benefited them not to do so. How can this be the case? You ask after everything I have said. Well, I will show you.

There are a number of things we must first understand to explain how and why Jessica died. One is Jessica herself. Jessica was a young, happy, carefree girl. She was a student living her best life. Her personality and character are of vital importance here. They are the key to understanding both how and why she died.

Let's first consider her knowledge of Kate and Tony's affair. How she found this out, neither of them knew. But when Kate and Jessica are talking, Kate discovers she does.

Jessica talks about an affair. About telling the truth and doing what is right. How guilty you feel if you do not.

You know, something has puzzled me about this. It is that this is out of character. Nothing I have heard about Jessica. Or anything in my own experience of her. This has led me to think that she would react this way in this situation. She is emotional. She is passionate. An impulsive artist. She wears her heart on her sleeve. And so, when she finds out her uncle is having an affair with her best friend. Does she merely imply it? Talking about it calmly? No. I believe that if Jessica had known that her best friend was cheating on her aunt with her uncle, she would be furious. She would be raging and screaming and shouting. So, what does her reaction mean? Well, it means that she did not know about your affair. But if this is the case, then why did she talk about an affair, truth, guilt? The answer is simple. She was talking about herself.

She was having an affair. She felt guilty for loving this man. And she wanted to tell the truth. She was not telling you that she knew of your affair. She was talking about her guilty conscience and how her heart was torn between her love and the truth.

This is also supported by a conversation she had with me before the party. At first, I assumed she was just asking me about her cousin. When she talked about the use of therapy to help someone feel remorse, I think she was. But after, when she asked about using therapy to deal with guilt. Then, I think she was talking about herself.

The next question, of course, is, Who was she having an affair with?" A nervous air filled the room. Eyes darting around to each other. "To determine this, we must first establish the lie they told to protect themselves. But that was ultimately the thing that gave them away."

Sebastien turned round. "When we were talking earlier. You said you attended the opening of the new sports centre in Exeter. Didn't you, Tony?"

Tony looked at him nervously. "Yes," He said with a faked confidence. Containing a hint of suspicion.

"Six months ago?" Sebastien asked.

"Yes, that is correct," Tony replied.

"Excellent," said Sebastien, smiling. "You see, that then leads us to our next question. How could someone have used a sports centre before it had even opened? Richard?"

Sebastien rotated to face Richard. Everyone's eyes fixed upon him.

"What? I don't know what you mean?"

"Oh, I think you do. You see, at the party, we were discussing St Sidwell's. You said you had swum there. But, earlier in the day. Whilst talking to Archie. You said you had not been to Exeter in years. So, the question remains, how can you have swum somewhere before it has even opened?"

Richard was lost for words. His breathing became more rapid. His face became red. His eyes darted frantically around the room.

"No answer?" Sebastien confirmed. "No matter. Let me do it for you. The truth is obviously that you were lying. Why?

Because you met Jessica there. Because it was you who was having an affair with her."

"Lies!" Richard shouted.

"NO!" Sebastien shot back. "This is the truth. You and Jessica had an affair. You met her in Exeter recently. She had told me she had seen the theatre in Exeter recently when she was seeing a 'friend.' But that was a lie. Really, she was seeing you. You two were having an affair. An affair that Jessica clearly wanted to expose.

As she had said. She wanted to tell the truth. To do the right thing. That her guilt was becoming too much. And no wonder. She was cheating on her cousin. But she loved you. So, she also wanted you for herself. So, telling the truth could achieve all of these things. But I don't think this is how you saw it. To you, I think this was just meant to be a bit of fun. She was merely your bit on the side, as they say. You did not love her. You were merely using her. And now you've had enough. And she was threatening to bring your life all tumbling down... At the worst possible time.

You see, the signs are all there. Samantha's cravings for sausages at the party. Her sickness the morning afterwards. Her hysterical reaction after the murder and on other occasions since. Which is so out of character. And even simply that she was not drinking alcohol at the party. Samantha is pregnant. You are having a baby. And this is why you killed Jessica.

Think about it. Samantha would soon tell her family about her pregnancy. Possibly even this weekend. She does not see them often. Once Jessica heard of this. Her mind would be made up. The guilt of letting her cousin start a family with a man who has betrayed her would intensify. Her fear of losing the man she loved to his new family would deepen. Yes, you knew she would tell Samantha everything. And that was something you could not allow. You knew Samantha would leave you. Breaking up your family and pushing away your true love. You knew you had to kill her.

So then comes the question of how you did it. As I said, only four people could have poisoned Jessica's glass before she drank from it. And you were not one of them. But that was my mistake. You see, Jessica never consumed the poison from her drink. Let's go back to the victim herself.

You see, Jessica had two hobbies which were vital for this plan to work. First, she liked to act. She was into amateur dramatics, but apparently, she was rather good. Secondly, she liked to play pranks. She had done so since she was a child. These two facts then gave you an opportunity—an opportunity for you to kill her in a way that no one thought you could have done.

Let's imagine that Richard had an idea. That Jessica should pretend to be poisoned at the party for a joke. Take a drink and act as if she were choking and fitting. Then, a few minutes later, it revealed that it was all an act. Well, why not? Jessica loved to act and play pranks. She would have found the idea exciting. And why would she think there was anything sinister? She is a carefree, bubbly young woman who loves him. She adored this man. She would never think he would want to hurt her. Unfortunately, she suspected nothing.

Perhaps she also felt a certain satisfaction at pulling this stunt at her cousin's party. After all, it is clear she thought Rebecca had acted badly. She knew Rebecca was not feeling the guilt that she should have felt. So perhaps Jessica felt Rebecca deserved this on her big day. And so, the stage was set.

Jessica takes a drink. Then, she starts to act. She pretends to choke, to struggle to breathe. She then falls over and pretends to have a fit. Once this starts, Richard springs into action. Once everyone's focus is fixed on Jessica, he goes to her abandoned glass. He puts some cyanide in her glass. Making us think that this is how she was poisoned. Then, while we are all focused on her face, he goes to her lower leg. There, he injects her with the cyanide. This then spreads through her bloodstream, causing her death within seconds." He paused. "Her symptoms had appeared before the poison had been administered."

Sebastien sighs. "The clues were all there. Archie told me that Richard was a farmer or something like that. Who in turn had heard this from his uncle. But then, when Samantha said she had met Richard in the hospital where she worked, I thought. Could he be a pharmacist? Someone knowledgeable in the effects of drugs. And experienced in the giving of injections. Then there is the syringe. When we saw Samantha, she thought she had packed five syringes, not four. She was right. Richard had taken one. And last night, after talking to Daniel, I found a burnt piece of cloth in the fire. It was this cloth that Richard had used to press on the wound to stop any bleeding before he disposed of it into the flames. The syringe he disposed of very cleverly. He breaks a glass and the syringe with it. Disposing of it right under my very nose. And then there was his position.

You see when you know that this was how she was poisoned. Then only he could have done it. All the rest of us were around her upper body. Focused on her face. Whereas he was the only person by her lower body. Holding her leg.

Jessica even showed some clues herself. First, her arm. She feels the effect of the poison enough to fall over, but she still thinks to put her arm out to break her fall. And then her reaction. You see her breathing, choking, fitting. There was a clear change. A point where it became more intense, more violent. Where it escalated from mild to deadly, this was the moment where the real poison was taking hold. It was the transition from a fake reaction to a real one. It was at that point that she was dying."

He turned to face Richard. His face is as hard as a stone. "You planned it all. For Jessica to pretend to be poisoned and then to inject her with real poison after all. You ruthlessly calculated how to kill this innocent young woman without incriminating yourself, disposing of the evidence, and framing Luke. But there was one thing you could not dispose of. You see, just an hour ago, I called the inspector. I asked him to ask the pathologist to examine the lower leg of Jessica for a tiny puncture mark. A mark that they found. A mark which proved you killed her."

The whole room was silent in shock. All their eyes were either fixed on Richard, their eyes raised in horror. Or looking out into space. Stunned by all that they had just heard. Everyone but Samantha. She just looked around frantically before focusing on Sebastien.

"This is nonsense. Absolute rubbish. Richard is not a murderer. Go on. Tell them," She urged him. But as she turned towards him, she realized. Looking at him. The man she had loved. Who she had married. She knew it was all true. She could see it in him. She knew him better than anyone. "Oh god!" She winced, turning away.

"No, baby," Richard pleaded desperately. "It's not true. It wasn't me. Please, you must believe me. I would never do that. Please. You know me. I love you," But it was no use. He had lost her. She knew what he had done.

He turned to Sebastien. His face twisted with anger. The rage and hatred boiled up within him. At this man who had ruined it all. Who had taken his perfect plan and had destroyed his life. He leapt up and ran towards him. All sense is now gone. Now, he just wanted revenge. He was within a meter of him when he felt a solid mass slamming into his lower body. He crashed to the floor in the grip of a police officer. Struggling with no use as he was restrained and cuffed. And with that, it was over.

CHAPTER 39

"So, it was when Uncle Tony mentioned Exeter? That was when you worked it all out?"

Sebastien and Archie were currently in a taxi, taking them to their train. It had been rather awkward leaving Claytons. Samantha was still in her room. Still distraught. Having lost her cousin was bad enough. But losing her husband as well. With a baby on the way. Her despair was completely understandable. But she would heal. With time, she would move on. Forgetting the man whose love for her had driven him to murder.

Then there was Tony. Both he and Imogen seemed distant since the arrest. Tony's betrayal breaking their marriage. When we said goodbye before leaving, the tension between them was clear. The atmosphere was unbearable.

The rest of the guests left at the same time we did. Kate left as soon as the arrest was made. Clearly, she could not stand to remain at Clayton's a second longer. Now that her secret had been exposed. Both Luke and Daniel left not soon after.

Now, thankfully, on their way back to London. Sebastien and Archie were discussing the case.

"Well, when he mentioned St Sidwell's. Yes," Sebastien replied. "There were certain thoughts I had before that point. But it was that final piece that made it all make sense."

"What other thoughts?" Archie asked.

"Well, why Cyanide? From the start, that did not make sense. As I said, the murderer had trapped themselves. They had narrowed down the list of suspects. And the time in which the poison could have been administered. Why had they done that? It only increased the likelihood they would be caught. The same applies to the location of the murder. The party. They could have chosen another location. One where they could not been present when the poison was consumed. Choosing the party, and that moment in the huddle did nothing but make them more identifiable. So why had they done that? Then, Jessica's response to Kate's affair. Again, it did not make sense. It did not fit her nature. Her best friend and Uncle cheat on her Aunty. The woman who has cared for her since her parent's death. No, her reaction would not be calm. It would be furious. She was a passionate, lively, impulsive young woman. No, again, it did not make sense. What we knew did not explain either of these facts. That cyanide was used, that she was poisoned at the party and that Jessica reacted in that way."

"And so, what Uncle Tony said explained that?"

"Well, no, not directly. But it did show us something. It showed us that Richard was lying. Once we knew that, all the rest fell into place. It enabled us to find an explanation that accounted for the three facts we mentioned before. It explained why the Cyanide was used as he needed a fast-acting poison. The symptoms needed to appear while Jessica was acting. It explained why she was poisoned at the party because it gave him the opportunity to create an alibi for himself with witnesses. As we all saw, he could not have poisoned her glass. And then her reaction. Because it was not a reaction at all, it was her talking about her relationship with Richard. Once I knew these facts, the other clues filled in the remaining gaps. Samantha's pregnancy. Which I did suspect but thought was irrelevant before. The burned cloth. The smashed glass. The missing syringe. The sudden escalation of her symptoms. The unusual position Richard took when she died. This explained it all!"

Archie exhaled deeply. "Well, I just don't get how you put it all together. It was just all so subtle."

Sebastien shrugged. "Well, I suppose you just pick things up, I guess. And at least I now know one thing."

"What's that?"

"Never to go to a family event of yours again!"

"Oh, come on, Admit it. You enjoyed it," Archie challenged. Sebastien looked at him. Puzzled. "Solving the murder, I mean."

Sebastien considered this for a second before shrugging.

"Maybe I enjoyed the challenge, I suppose. But still, I would prefer it if the next place we went to together was the pub."

"Oh, I agree with that." Said Archie with a smile. "At least you can watch your precious Bake Off when we get back."

Sebastien smiled. "Ah, yes. I am looking forward to that."

"Out of curiosity, what cake are you eating when you watch it?"

Sebastien looked at him suspiciously. "Victoria Sponge, why?"

"Well, I do fancy some cake."

"Oh, so you're inviting yourself to my Bake-Off session now?" Sebastien asked.

"Yes," Said Archie hesitantly.

Sebastien looked at him seriously. "Yeah, alright then." He replied, cracking a smile. "But you have to bring your own cake!"

"Oh, I've got that covered," Archie said smugly.

"Let me guess, chocolate?"

"Nope," said Archie with satisfaction. "Lemon drizzle"

"Oh yes, that sounds good. Just make sure you don't put any almonds in it."

Archie twisted suddenly and looked at Sebastien straight in the face.

"I'm just saying."